KILL ME

KISS OF DEATH #1

LP LOVELL

D1557371

1

UNA

I bump my bike over the curb and allow it to roll down the small embankment into the tree line. Kicking the stand down, I take off my helmet and my hair falls loose down my back. The scent of the woods wraps around me, the pine trees, the earth, the moss. After the confines of the city, it's a welcome reprieve that revitalizes me. The city is too loud, the cars, the people, it both overwhelms and numbs my senses. Out here, I can hear everything and nothing, because silence reigns, disturbed only by the occasional chitter of a bird.

Pulling my hood up over my head, I start jogging up the road, clinging to the shadows as I approach the house. To the unsuspecting person, this is merely the Hamptons mansion of some guy with a fuck lot of money, I know better. This is the fortress of Arnaldo Boticelli, the under-boss of the Italian Mafia. Not many outsiders will ever see the inside of those walls, and I am always an outsider. It's why they hire me.

I wait until the guards change; taking advantage of their small moment of distraction to make for the six-foot high stone pillar that sits to the left of the enormous metal gate, just in the shadow of the guardhouse. Gripping the ledge, I haul myself up, launching straight over the top and landing on the other side in a silent roll. Pausing, my senses pick up the slightest sound and movement. The faint panting of a dog and the clumsy footfalls of heavy boots are all I hear. Thirty seconds is all I have to get to the house. I run over the dark lawns, but the closer I get, the riskier it is. The mansion is like a modern palace, made of glass walls that allow light to spill out across all that surrounds it. There are at least three snipers on the roof along with four guard patrols circling the perimeter and six directly surrounding the house.

Scanning the house, I spot one of the upstairs guest rooms has a window that is ajar. The enormous pane of glass is tilted from a central pivot, and the room behind it is cast in darkness, one of the few that isn't lit up like a Christmas tree. The guard below the window seems distracted, bored. Making a break for it, my feet whisper across the grass as I run up behind him, jumping and wrapping my thighs around his hips in order to leverage my arm around his throat. He staggers for a moment and slams back into the wall. I squeeze harder, using everything I have to crush his thick neck. And then he goes down, hitting the ground with a soft thud.

Now...I just need to scale the building and slip in the second-storey window. Easy.

A few minutes later and I'm peering around a wall at Arnaldo's office doors. Two guards stand outside, both armed. Yanking my hood further down, I step out from behind the wall. The guards snap their attention to me, and I pop just a little more sway in my hips as I approach them. They both reach for their weapons and I drop to the ground, ripping the pistols from my thigh holsters and pulling them up in front of me. The triggers give way under my index fingers with a silenced pop. Both of them grapple for a second, reaching for the small darts protruding from their necks before they simultaneously slide to the floor. Darts so aren't my style, but then it doesn't go over well to come into a client's house and kill their personal guards. I press my boot against the arm of one of the guys, shoving him to the side so I can open the door. My boots sink into the thick carpet and I push the door closed behind me.

Arnaldo looks up from his enormous desk and smiles, steepling his fingers in front of him. Of course, he was expecting me. I told him I was coming. Two more guards stand like silent vigils behind him, their backs straight and their assault rifles pointed at me. I keep my face lowered towards the ground, ensuring that the hood casts my face in shadow.

"You going to shoot me, boys?" When in the worst situations, I often find a smile can save you. Everything in life is about perception. What you do doesn't matter, only your opponent's perception of what you will do. Smile when they expect you to cower, play the helpless woman when they expect you to come out all guns blazing. An unpredictable enemy is deadly, after all.

"Una," Arnie greets me in his thick Italian accent before clicking his fingers, signalling for his men to leave. He knows I won't talk with them here. The door clicks shut behind them, and he gestures for me to sit. "Thank you for agreeing to meet."

I'm already aware of the man behind me in the corner of the room, but I'm waiting to see if he'll move. Arnaldo is the one who gives it away, his eyes shifting infinitesimally before meeting mine again. Smiling, I drop the tiny silver blade from the thick cuff around my right wrist. It's the size of a large hairpin, but as sharp as a razor and weighted to have a reasonable throwing range. My hand flies out behind me as I keep my eyes fixed on Arnaldo. I hear the blade drive home, burying itself into the wood of the door with a soft thud. The mob boss's lips curl in the shadow of a smile.

"You missed." The voice behind me is rough and deep. He approaches from behind, and I fight to stay still when I feel him brush entirely too close. Circling in front of me, he stops, our bodies barely an inch apart. The aim is to intimidate, and it amuses me. He's tall, a lot taller than me, but where most of the men Arnaldo keep seem to be bulky, this one is athletic. His shoulders are broad, tapering into a narrow waist. Honed muscles lay over his lithe frame, the result of discipline and work. Some women see a man like this and think him attractive, but I'm beyond such base notions. I think him dangerous. He stands casually, his hands in the pockets of the expensive suit that wraps around his body like a glove. He radiates power like a beacon, it unfurls, curling around me and sucking all the air from the room. My curiosity wins out and I tip my head back, dragging my eyes up his chest until they reach his face. He looks like one of those guys you see in a magazine. Full lips, chiseled jaw, high cheekbones, and hair that's just slightly too long to be professional. Everything about him screams entitled, rich, pretty boy, until I look in his eyes. They're the colour of a well-aged whisky and almost completely unreadable, ice cold. I fight to keep a smile off my lips, because everything about him screams challenge. His eyes narrow and I see the tight restraint, the leash he puts himself on, because there's an edge to him, something cold and dangerous with a ruthlessness to rival my own. He catches me off guard for the smallest of moments, but it's enough, because he's seen my face. I'm not entirely upset at the notion, because it means I might have to kill him, and this one would make for an exciting adversary.

Reaching up, I brush my finger over the shell of his ear, coating my finger in the blood pooling from the small knick. "I never miss." His eyes hold me captive as I lift the finger to my lips and suck, tasting the coppery tang of him. He doesn't flinch, doesn't move. "If I wanted you dead, you'd be dead." His expression never wavers, never gives away even a hint of what he's thinking. He's both intriguing and infuriating.

"Bacio della morte," he says in fluent Italian, his tongue caressing the words like a lover.

Kiss of death. It's what the Italians call me.

"Sei spaventato?" I reply with a smirk. *Are you scared?* I can't help but bait him, though I doubt this one fears anything. You know what they say, there's a fine line between bravery and stupidity. He'll find it's a very fine line indeed when dealing with me.

Tilting his head to the side, a stray lock of dark hair falls across his forehead. The move reminds me of a predator weighing its prey, which is laughable. His eyes hold mine long past the point where normal people would start to feel uncomfortable. The way he looks at me almost has me wanting to look away, to back down. *Me!* I never back down from anyone, because to do so is to perceive a threat. No one threatens me. Who is this man? He embodies power, wears it like a man who was born with it, and yet, I do not know him, which means he does not assume power. Curious. Everyone can be read like facts off a sheet of paper, their fears, their hopes, their strengths, their weaknesses…if you know what to look for, they'll tell you everything. He's telling me nothing, giving away nothing, and it has me intrigued. I stare into his eyes, pushing, probing, looking, and yet he stands like a wall of iron in front of me, impenetrable and steadfast.

Eventually, I tear my eyes from his and walk past him dismissively. An uneasy feeling crawls through my gut at having my back to him, my instincts warning me that this one is dangerous, but survival and domination are as much about the bluff as anything else. To acknowledge him as a worthy adversary in itself lends him power that I am not willing to give, because I am the danger here, and if he makes a move, regardless of who he is, he will soon learn why.

I round the desk and Arnaldo hefts his weight from his chair, pulling me into a hug and kissing both my cheeks. The Italians have their ways and they get upset if you piss in their cornflakes, so I play along, despite the fact that the brush of his skin against mine has long ingrained instincts roaring to the surface. I liken it to a lion throwing itself against the bars of a cage, overcome with the primal instinct to kill. But I have forged a prison of tempered steel that keeps my monster firmly locked up, chained and hidden from the world until I need her. He pulls away and I release the breath I'd been holding. Arnie's a bear of a man, who always smells of cigars and whisky, but he's a loyal client, and I value loyalty.

"Arnie, it's been a while," I say casually. He sits back down and offers me a drink he knows I won't take, followed by the chair he knows I'll refuse to sit in. I've worked with him for four years. He knows well enough.

"I'm happy to say I haven't needed your services of late." I move, leaning my back against the wall, off to the side of Arnie's desk.

I glance at tall, dark and handsome. He's standing in the same position, only now he's facing us. His hands are still in his pockets, giving the perception of casual relaxation, but nothing about that man is casual. He's aware, watching, waiting. A frown shadows his features as he assesses me.

"He needs to leave," I say, tilting my head towards him.

Arnie sighs and leans back in his chair. "This concerns him. Plus, I don't trust you not to kill me." He grins.

"Oh, Arnie." I smile sweetly, slipping my fingers beneath the thin hood and pushing it back off my face. "It's cute that you think anyone could protect you if I wanted you dead." His face becomes serious as I move to his desk, swaying my hips with every step. "Don't worry. I'd want at least twenty for you." I wink. Like I said, this game is all about perception. Confidence is a must, and charm goes a long way. I'm not one for bullshit. I'd happily never interact with a client face-to-face, but Arnie is one I make an exception for. Even he must remember his place though, because mob boss, cartel leader, motherfucking president...death doesn't discriminate, she sells to the highest bidder.

2

NERO

The way she walks, the way she speaks, the way she toys with Boticelli has me more interested than I should be. I know little about her, but I can tell one thing, she can't be controlled. The stories about her are well known, the Russian assassin who took out Salvatore Carosso, a key player in the Mexican Cartel. If I saw her on the street, I wouldn't look at her twice. And that, I realise, is why she's so good. On the outside she looks like a pretty little thing full of empty threats, but one look in her eyes has me weighing her very differently, because there's nothing there. No emotion, no doubt, no conscience.

She approaches Boticelli's desk, and I watch the muscle in his jaw twitch at her thinly veiled threat, and yet, he says nothing. He does nothing. She has the underboss of the Italian mob biting his tongue like a whipped dog. The corner of my lip twitches as I try not to smile. He's scared of her. His eyes dart to me, as though I'll save him. I won't. He's a means to an end, but I have fuck all loyalty to him beyond what he can do for me. It's her I need. She hops up on the edge of his desk, facing me and crosses one leg over the other, swinging her boot back and forth as if she doesn't have a care in the world. She braces her hands behind her, stretching her lean body out and thrusting her chest forward. The material of her top pulls tight over her chest, and my eyes trace the length of her body. White-blonde hair falls down her back in waves, making her milky skin appear even more pale. Yeah, I can see why she's so good, because if I didn't know who she was, I'd be all too willing to sink my dick in her. She's like killer Barbie. She's perfect.

"Fine. You want to talk in front of him, do, but…" She swings her gaze towards me, narrowing those unusual indigo coloured eyes at me. "Betray me, and I will find you."

There are two types of people in this world, those who threaten and those who promise. I always appreciate people who make promises. Her eyes lock with mine, and I stare back at her wordlessly. Little does she know that to speak of this situation would damage me a lot more than it would her. She'll find that out soon enough though.

"Okay." Arnie huffs impatiently. "This is your mark."

He hands her a file and she opens it, skimming over the page before closing it and discarding it on the desk beside her. "Three," she says simply.

The boss narrows his eyes. "Three million? He's a capo."

She tilts her head back and then rolls her neck to the side, looking at him with a bored expression on her face. "He is not just a capo. He's Lorenzo Santos. I need time to get close to him, and time is money, Arnie."

Fucking Lorenzo. He's an idiot with his dick in his hand. She'd only have to look at him and he'd blindly follow her to a slit throat.

Arnaldo grins like a shark and picks up the half

smoked cigar from the ashtray on his desk. He takes a lighter from his pocket and flips the top, allowing the flame to kiss the blackened end of the cigar. He puffs on it a couple of times and exhales a heavy cloud of smoke.

"Getting close won't be a problem. That's what Nero here is for." He jerks the cigar towards me and ash falls on the desk, scattering across the wood. Una's eyes lock with mine, focused, studying. "Santos is throwing an engage-ment party in two week's time and you will be his date." The boss adds.

She knows just as well as I do that security that night will be even tighter than normal. She might get in, but she sure as shit won't be getting out. It's a suicide mission. And a test. Arnaldo thinks that our interests are one and the same, that this is a simple takeover. It's not, but for now, I need him on my side. More importantly, I needed him to put me in contact with the best hitman money can buy... or hitwoman. Una Ivanov. She's elusive and completely impossible to contact unless you're in the know. Arnaldo is in the know. The pieces are on the chessboard, I just need to put them into play.

She inhales deeply, her nostrils flaring. "Fine, but it's still three mil."

She hops off the desk and walks towards me. Her hips sway delicately, her body moving like liquid art. Coming to a halt in front of me, she lifts a hand, trailing perfectly manicured nails over my jaw. I wrap a hand around her wrist, halting her movement. I don't trust her for shit. A smile curls the corners of her blood red lips, and I squeeze her wrist hard enough to bruise her porcelain skin, hard enough that I know with a tiny bit more pressure I could break the delicate bones. Her eyes flash with something, but she never flinches, never moves, never stops smiling. We simply stare at each other.

"What was your name again?" Her expression shifts, interest shining in her eyes.

"Nero."

"Nero...?" I hesitate and her smirk widens into a full grin. "I will find out, so save me the time and the addition to Arnie's bill."

I have no doubt she will have my life story in a matter of hours. "Verdi," I say. She gives no reaction, no response at all.

"A nobody," she says quietly. "Curious."

"A nobody." I agree. I plaster a smirk on my face and release her wrist, trailing my fingers over her arm. She stiffens for the briefest second, but I catch it.

She presses her body against mine and her breath blows over my jaw, her eyes dropping to my lips as she tilts her head to the side. I'm sure many a man has been lured to his death by that tight body and those full lips. I'm not one of them. I keep my eyes on hers, waiting.

"And yet here you are, cosied up to the boss," she whispers, cocking an eyebrow. "High stakes for a nobody." Clever girl. She bites down on one side of her bottom lip. "I like you, Nero." She smoothes her palm over the front of my jacket, before slipping away from me. "I think you'd be hard to kill, and I do so love a challenge." She smiles and winks before she walks to the door leisurely, as though she has all the time in the world. Pausing, she pulls her hood up again, until only her white-blonde hair spills over her shoulder, and then she's gone.

The game is officially in play.

———

INHALING THE SMOKE, I hold it, allowing it to burn my lungs before I release it. I'm about a mile away from

Lorenzo's house, parked in the driveway of an empty house with a real estate sign outside. Una is precisely three minutes late.

I look up when a black Mercedes comes hurtling down the street. It slows and pulls into the drive beside my car before the engine cuts out. It takes me a second to realise who it is, because her long, white-blonde hair is now dark brown and skimming her jaw line. The door opens and Una's lithe frame unfolds from the car. Her body is covered in a red dress that masks any trace of her skin and yet clings to every single curve she has. If her aim is to distract and seduce then I can't imagine she'll have a problem. The woman is a siren. Death wrapped in a bow.

"Nice dress." I push off the hood of my car, throwing the cigarette on the ground.

She barely even spares me a glance. "Smoking will kill you," she says, moving to the passenger side.

"I'd say it's the least of our worries right now." I open the driver's door and slide into the leather seat.

She gets in and closes the door behind her. "Speak for yourself. Risk is calculated and directly related to your level of skill."

"Arrogance will get you killed." I reverse out of the drive, fishtailing the car onto the road with a flick of the steering wheel.

She lets out a short laugh. "I'm the best, Mr Verdi. It's not arrogance, simply fact." She takes a small mirror out of her bag and checks her lipstick. The red matches her dress and contrasts dramatically with her pale skin. "I don't take jobs that will get me killed."

"So you have a plan to get out?" Arnaldo told me before not to ask questions and let her do what he hired her for, but this isn't Arnaldo's show, no matter how much he might think himself the puppeteer. I wish I could be the one to end Lorenzo, so I could smile over his dying body and watch his worthless life drain from him. But I need to remain distanced from this.

"You read the file I sent?"

"Yeah, but there wasn't much to go on." She sent me a file detailing her fake identity as well as vague details about said identity. That's it. "You're aware of the heightened security?"

I glance at her when she doesn't respond and see the corner of her lips curled up, sinking a small dimple into her cheek. "There was as much as you need to play your part. Don't question my methods, and I won't question why you want your brother dead." I turn my attention back to the road, tightening my grip on the steering wheel and clenching my jaw. Of course she would find out that Lorenzo is my brother. I feel her gaze touch the side of my face, but deliberately refuse to look her way.

"Half-brother," I say through gritted teeth. "And I have my reasons."

"You make the mistake of thinking I actually care."

"I need to know how this is going to play out. I can't be culpable." My voice lowers until it's barely above a growl.

She sighs dramatically. "We walk in together. Shortly after we arrive, I'll slip away. Your brother will follow me, job done. You won't see me afterwards so don't wait around."

"You really think you're going to make it out?"

She laughs, a light tinkling sound that contradicts her completely. "I know I am. You should worry about yourself. The girl you brought to the party kills your brother... that won't go down well for you."

"I have that under control." I hate my brother and he hates me, but he's the capo and I'm a good enforcer. Our feud isn't publicly known. As far as everyone is concerned,

I'm the loyal brother, willing to kill for Lorenzo. The only ones who know any different are my closest guys, Tommy, Gio and Jackson. I suspect Lorenzo has kept it the same; after all, rifts in the family make it look weak. But then, he never was the sharpest, so I could be wrong. By the time anyone is brave enough to voice their suspicions, I'll be capo. They're scared of me now; they'll be terrified of me then.

When I pull up to the house there are a line of cars waiting to get up the driveway. The parking is on one of the lawns outside the gates, and people are waiting on foot as Lorenzo's soldiers pat down guests upon entry.

Una smoothes a hand over her wig and throws the door open. Reaching out, I grab her arm to stop her, but before I can she rips away from my grasp and slams the same arm across my throat. My Adam's apple hits the back of my throat and I choke for a second, my vision dotting. It takes me a couple of precious seconds without oxygen to move. My instinct is to grab the back of her head and smash it against the dash, but that wouldn't do much for her face, and I need her intact for this job. Instead, I grip her wrist and squeeze, hard enough to shove her an inch away from me. She may be fast, but she's tiny and I'm infinitely stronger. She pulls her arm away from me, tucking it back against her side. Her nostrils flare, pupils dilated. Her fists clench and release repeatedly as she tries to gather control of herself.

"I need you right now, but do that again and I'll put a bullet in that pretty little head of yours," I growl, trying to leash my temper. I don't like surprises, and I certainly don't like being bested. Cracking my neck from side to side in an attempt to dislodge the ache deep in my throat.

She turns to face me, those indigo eyes locking with mine. Something shifts between us, the threat of violence pulsing like a living thing. "If you value your life, do not ever touch me when I'm unawares."

"What I was attempting to do was to warn you that they will frisk you. If they find even your handy blade there, it will fuck everything." I point at the thick silver cuff around her wrist.

She turns away, perching on the edge of the seat. "That information really wasn't worth getting injured for," she drawls, that hint of a Russian accent creeping in where she usually hides it so well.

I laugh. "Duly noted." She thinks she's bulletproof because she incites fear. She has no power here because she relies on the most basic animal instinct. Survival. People will do whatever they have to in order to survive and so fear becomes a valuable ally. I learned a long time ago that surviving is not living, so I will either get what I want or die trying. I always get what I want.

We approach the gate, waiting in line with the other guests. Nero slides his hand around my waist, resting it on my hip. I grit my teeth but make a concerted effort to keep my gaze forward and a smile on my lips. I'm a killer, but above all else, I'm an actress. I can be anyone, assume any role or identity given to me, because killing someone is the easy part. It's getting close that's the problem, and trust me, when you go after the kind of people I do, you want to be close before you take a shot at them. They have a habit of dodging bullets and shooting back. His fingers wrap around my hip, gripping me more firmly.

"You're brave," I growl under my breath. His fingers twitch and the heat from his palm seeps through the material of my dress, branding my skin.

He huffs a laugh. "Maybe I just have complete faith in your ability to be professional."

"Hmm." I smile at one of the guards who glances my way as he's patting down the woman in front of us. I trail my hand up my body until my fingers cover his, gently wrapping them around his hand. I squeeze and he lets out a low grunt. "How professional do you think you'll be when I break your hand?" I hiss, smiling sweetly at him for the sake of our audience.

He leans in, smirking as he brushes a finger over my cheek. "Now, now, *Isabelle*. You'll make me hard before my pat-down." He leans in close until his lips are at my ear. "I do so love a violent streak in a woman."

And I do so love making men bleed. On a job I'm focused, in control, and yet, something about him makes everything in me want to rise to the challenge he constantly throws down simply by existing. To anyone looking at us, we must look like a couple that is so in love they can't keep their hands off each other. Perception is everything. I squeeze his hand harder and watch the strain flash across his face. He pulls back slightly, and I slowly release him, keeping my eyes fixed on him as his fingers trail over my hip, caressing the top of my ass.

The couple in front of us move away and we step up to the guards.

"Hold your arms out to the side," one says robotically to me. I do as told and take a deep breath as his hands sweep over my body. He moves onto Nero while the other guy runs a bug scanner over me. Of course it never goes off. I have all the tools I need to kill Lorenzo on my person, but nothing that could possibly be so easily detected or even so much as suspected. When they're done, Nero smiles and wishes them a good day in Italian before placing his hand at the small of my back.

"Before you threaten to dislocate my shoulder, remember we're a couple, *Morte*. And trust me, the more I look like I want you, the more my brother will want you." His voice drops and though nothing this man says should affect me, it strangely does, just enough to draw my attention to the fact.

"Well, you Italian boys do like to keep it in the family."

He ignores me as we pass through the high stone walls that surround the garden courtyard at the back of the house. The property reminds me of a traditional Tuscany villa, with the terracotta tiled roof and the flowers growing up the side of the enormous house. As soon as we walk into the courtyard, people greet Nero. Again, his name doesn't hold much weight, and I can see that in the way people approach him, and yet that effortless power of his seems to win out. They quickly drop their gaze when he speaks, even older, Made men who owe him no such respect. It's not respect though, it's impulse, an instinctual reaction they can't help. Nicholai would love him. He'd rise in the bratva fast with that kind of ability. The Italians are stupid though. Ability means nothing against bloodlines. The last I checked, the fact that your father fucked your mother wasn't a reason to garner respect, but that is the Italian way.

As per the file, he introduces me as Isabelle Jacobs, an all-American girl he's 'dating', just until the family finds a well-bred Italian girl and demand he marry her of course. Traditions again. I'm treated as all women are treated in the mafia, like a pretty ornament whose sole worth is in my ability to spread my legs. In my line of work, I have found that the underestimation and quick dismissal of women works in my favour.

We've been here twenty minutes when I spot Lorenzo, and when I do, I find him already watching me. His fiancée is on his arm. She can be no more than twenty, and she looks terrified. Well, I'm about to save her from an arranged marriage. I hold Lorenzo's stare for a beat, and when he doesn't look away, I flash him a small smirk before dropping my gaze as if I'm shy. When I look back up, his attention has shifted slightly to Nero on my left. The look in his eye is pure animosity. Nero has three older guys eating out of the palm of his hand, laughing and talking in Italian, another move to exclude me from the conversation. Of course, I understand every word they're saying. I pull away from Nero's side and he offers me a brief glance, a frown marring his features. I make a show of seeming pissed off and storm away. I approach the small open bar, pushing past the cluster of wives that are standing by it, delicately clasping their champagne glasses.

The waiter behind the bar smiles politely, resembling a little penguin in his tuxedo. "Vodka on ice," I tell him. He pours the clear liquid into the glass, the ice cracking under the alcohol as he slides it across to me.

"A woman who likes the hard stuff."

A slow smile pulls at my lips as I turn to face the owner of the subtly accented voice. Lorenzo isn't quite as tall as his brother and he certainly doesn't carry the air of power, despite the fact that he's capo. He has the same dark hair and deep brown eyes, the same chiselled cheekbones and jaw line, coupled with a set of lips that I'm sure make most women fall all over themselves. And yet, Nero is somehow just more in every way, speaking from a completely objective standpoint, of course.

"Always." I lift the glass to my lips and take a sip, locking eyes with him over the rim of the glass.

He turns, bracing his back against the bar and allowing his eyes to roam over the guests gathered in the garden. "How do you know my brother?"

"I fuck him." Titters erupt from the women behind me, and I smile. Of course he catches it. He was supposed to. "I see you're more the settling type. Congratulations." His eyes drop to my lips. "I do love a wedding." I lower my voice and allow my gaze to roam over his body while biting my bottom lip. The look in his eyes is one I recognize all too well. The pulse point at his neck beats faster and his pupils dilate. His breathing picks up ever so slightly and he shifts on his feet, probably because his pants are becoming a bit uncomfortable. "Although, you don't look thrilled at the prospect." I rest my elbow on the bar and pop my hip, accentuating the curve of my body.

"Hmm, well, this world is full of so much temptation," he says each word carefully. "And you deserve a better offer than my brother." He almost hisses the words, as if the very notion offends him. The more he talks, the more the differences between Nero and he become painfully clear. Admittedly, Nero had the advantage of knowing what I was from the moment he met me. But Lorenzo's naivety, his assumption that I am exactly what I appear to be... well, it's disappointing. Or perhaps I'm just that good. After all, I was crafted for this very purpose, to be a chameleon, to blend in and become whatever it is my prey wants me to be. Right now, he wants me to be the hot chick that his brother is sleeping with. He wants to fuck me and stick it to Nero. I step forward, closing the gap between us.

"So make me a better offer." I raise an eyebrow and focus on his lips, which slowly curl into a satisfied grin.

That's all it takes for him to pick up my glass off the bar and down the remaining vodka before turning and walking away. Glancing across the courtyard garden to where Nero is talking in a small group, I know his attention has been firmly on me this entire time. His eyes lock with mine, narrowing, as his jaw tenses. Ignoring him, I follow Lorenzo out of the courtyard. He slips through a side gate, whispering something to the guard standing there as he passes. The guard nods, and when I approach him with a sensual smile gracing my lips, he steps to the side without a word. I leave some distance between us as I trace Lorenzo's path up the stone steps that lead to a sunroom attached to the back of the house. Inside, various plants creep over the glass and the scents of different flowers assault me. The sound of running water trickles over my senses. Most people would probably find it soothing, but for me it triggers a short burst of images to flash through my mind. Hands holding me down, panic, choking, drowning, catching a breath only to drown all over again. Snapping my focus back to the task at hand, I crack my neck from side to side and take a deep breath to centre myself again.

Lorenzo hooks left, under a small archway that leads into what I assume is the main house. He walks up the stairs and along a corridor before he stops at a door. He glances over his shoulder, flashing me a small smile as the heavy oak door opens with a groan.

The room is small with a couple of leather sofas in the middle and a desk at the back. I'm registering every possible threat, anything I can use as a weapon in the event that something goes wrong, and most importantly, an escape plan. There's the door I came in through of course, but that leads back into the house, which may be heavily guarded. At the back of the office are two narrow glass doors that lead out onto a stone balcony. That's my most likely escape route at this point.

The latch of the door clicks shut with a heavy finality and the silence it leaves behind is deafening, as though the world itself is suddenly holding its breath, waiting for death to strike.

Hands brush over the side of my neck, but I don't flinch this time, because I'm ready. I'm in the place in my mind where the kill, the lust for blood, goes beyond any uncomfortable feelings he may elicit. It's a side of myself that I hide, that I'm ashamed of, but not because of some misplaced guilt. Do not give me credit that is not due. I'm ashamed because I'm better than that. I was trained to be impassive, the elite, silent warrior. Death is a job, a necessity, we neither like nor dislike it, it just is. But for me, in a world where everything is a map of grey existence, this is my only spike of colour. It's when I take the ultimate prize from someone else that I am given a gift, a moment of relief, a moment of bliss. And the possibility of that moment excites me.

His lips brush over my skin so lightly that the hairs on the back of my neck prickle to attention. "Would you like a drink?" he murmurs.

I turn to face him, deliberately placing myself barely an inch away from him. I'm careful not to lean in, not to incite anything. Yet. I need him to get that drink first. "I'll have whatever you're having." His eyes flash with lust, and yet he holds his composure as he steps into the corner and starts pouring from the crystal decanter. Keeping my eyes fixed on him, I slide the diamond ring off my right index finger and use my thumbnail to dislodge the stone. Sliding the ring into my clutch bag, I keep the small stone in my hand. When he turns around with the drinks, I'm sitting on the edge of his desk with my legs crossed. His eyes move over my body as he hands me the glass. I place it to my lips and take a swig of the well-aged amber liquor. The sharp, smoky taste dances across my tongue, and I narrow my eyes at him, daring him closer. The second I put the glass down on the desk beside me, he makes a move, stepping towards me and wrapping a hand around the back of my neck.

"You're a beautiful woman, Isabelle."

I smile. "So, you know my name."

He smirks. "Of course." His lips slam over mine so

hard it takes me by surprise for a second, but just a split second. His glass is still clutched in his hand between us, and he's really making this too easy. I reach across the gap between us, brushing the edge of the glass and dropping the stone in his drink. It makes a small fizzing sound, but I grab the back of his neck and moan into his mouth, covering it easily. His tongue probes against my lips, seeking entrance, but instead I push him away. His eyebrows pull together in confusion.

"I think I need to finish my drink for what you're offering," I tease, scraping my teeth over my bottom lip and picking up my glass.

He huffs a low chuckle and lifts his own glass to his lips, taking a heavy gulp. I need him to finish it. Tipping mine back, I down the entire thing. He cocks a brow and takes another heavy gulp that leaves the glass almost empty. Good enough. And the effect is almost instant. He frowns and a soft cough works its way up his throat. I place my hands behind me on the desk and lean back. He coughs again, clutching at his throat.

"What…?" His gaze lifts to mine, and I see the exact moment when he realizes his error. He opens his mouth to shout, probably for a guard, but all that comes out is a choked sound. His chest heaves and a thin sheen of sweat coats his skin. His knees buckle, slamming into the hard tile floor with an unforgiving crack. And there he stays, a powerful man brought to his knees, left gasping and mumbling incoherently. I push off the desk and circle his prone form.

"Cyanide. Nasty stuff. It turns your own body against you, prevents your cells from absorbing oxygen." I tilt my head to the side, looking down at him. His eyes fix me in a glare that holds absolutely no weight given his current position. Dropping to a crouch in front of him, I grab his jaw, forcing him to look at me. "So while you're there, gasping for air, your body is suffocating from the inside." I smile and he stares at me as if he's going to survive this and hunt me to the ends of the earth. He wouldn't be the first to think so. The human mind is a strange animal and even at the last minute, when it knows it's lost, that the body it holds so dear is failing, it still hopes. The truth is, when pushed to the very edge of our survival, human beings are dreamers and fantasists by nature. No matter how much of a realist we are in life, death reveals all, taunting us with our own naïve brand of hope.

"Do you know who I am?" I ask, standing and moving around him slowly, leisurely. He doesn't answer, of course, what with the effort to breathe. "They call me bacio della morte." His eyes briefly flick to me before squeezing shut. "Arnaldo sends his regards." His teeth grit, and I know any minute his heart is going to give out. He pitches backwards and lands, sprawled awkwardly on the carpet. He's still breathing, but barely. His lungs are nothing more than a desperate quivering reflex of a failing body. Taking my lipstick and compact mirror from my clutch bag I apply a new coat, ensuring his messy kisses haven't smudged the last layer all over my face. The frantic beat of his lungs slows until only a few gasps remain, like a fish left out in the sun to die. And then it stops. His breath ceases and he slips into cardiac arrest. Dropping to my knees beside his body, I lean over him and wait for the tell-tale hiss of air leaving his lips.

"Prosti menya." *Forgive me.* I'm not a pious woman. I've seen too much evil in this world to ever believe in a god or anything greater than this hellhole of a life we have. This man did nothing to me; he's simply a job, a paid contract. He died because he was weak. I continue to survive because I am strong and do what I was trained to do. Kill.

I ask forgiveness because although I have to do this, I shouldn't enjoy it nearly as much as I do.

As always, I press my lips against his waxy forehead. Just then, the door opens and I leap to my feet, widening my stance and crouching like a cat ready to strike. I release a breath when I realize it's Nero. "Fucking knock!" I snap.

He glances from me to his brother's lifeless body on the floor. "I'm sorry. They're coming for you."

Well, fuck. No sooner has he said the words than I hear the fast approach of several men. The stairs groan under their weight, and I know if I stay here, I'm dead.

I go to yank open the glass doors, but they're locked. I pick up the heavy leather chair behind the desk with the intent of smashing the glass, but a single gunshot goes off before I can.

"Go! Run!" Nero hisses, glancing down the corridor and clutching Lorenzo's gun in his hand. He shot the glass out. Throwing myself through the narrow gap, my dress catching on the jagged glass that lines the doorframe. I'm on the first floor, and it's not that high, but it's no walk in the park either. I won't die, but if I break an ankle, then I might as well have, because if I can't run, I'm dead.

Another gunshot rings out, this one coming so close to me that I hear the sharp crack as it breaks the air next to my ear. I'm all for making this look authentic, but I swear to god, if he shoots me... Springing up onto the balcony, I launch myself into the air. There's a moment of complete weightlessness before I hit the grass, dropping into a roll of torn red satin. The logical thing would be to make for the treeline and hop the fence over the property line, but that's exactly why I'm not doing that. Ducking against the building, I press myself into the brickwork directly beneath the balcony. The voices above me are shouting orders, baying for my blood. Nero is right there, instructing them to

double the patrol on the fence line and not let anyone
leave. Ripping off the wig and pulling the pins from my
hair, I shake out my long strands. The dress is already
ruined, but I grab the material of the bodice and pull it
apart, shredding it down the middle until it pools at my
waist, revealing a pale blue sleeveless dress beneath. I step
out of the first dress and hook around the corner of the
building. Balling up the red material and the wig, I make
sure to hide them well at the base of a bush that sits against
the house. As I make my way towards the gardens, I pull
out a pair of sunglasses from my bag and slide them on.
My step falters only for a second when six armed men in
suits round the corner and start jogging straight
towards me.

"Ma'am, this area is off limits," the first one says, his
expression stern and unforgiving.

I glance at the gun in his hand and swallow heavily,
taking a shaky step to the side. All for show, of course.

"Oh, I'm sorry. I seem to have lost my boyfriend." I
push a tremor into my voice.

"Please go back to the party with the other guests." He
says dismissively.

I smile sweetly, like the nice, dutiful girlfriend. They
suspect nothing, because they're looking for a sexy,
murderous brunette in a red dress, and in this dress, well, I
could almost pull off sweet.

Rounding the sunroom at the back of the building, I
slip back through the gap in the wall. Keeping my gaze
fixed down as I pass the guard; although, this is a different
guy from when I passed by earlier. When I step into the
courtyard, the guests are visibly tense. The men are all
looking on edge, not helped by the fact that none of them
have any of their weapons to hand. For men like these,
being without a gun is like being naked. The women

huddle together nervously like the pathetic sheep they are, and I notice the strategic circle of men that surround them, as if they're some grand treasure they must protect. Everyone's attention seems to focus on me. That can't be good. A throat clears behind me, and I realize that it's not me they're focusing on, it's Nero. He stands behind me at the top of the steps that descend into the garden, the floral archway surrounding him and contrasting with the hard, dark lines of his face and body. I drop down a couple of steps, slipping out of sight of the gathered crowd.

"Ladies and gentlemen." His voice is a deep boom that I'm sure can be heard clearly by even those furthest away. "There is nothing to be concerned about, merely a small security issue." He smiles and it's so genuine, so confident, that even I find it soothing. "Please, let's enjoy the party while the guards handle it." He raises his full champagne glass, flashing a wide, perfect smile at the guests. There are a few murmurs, questions, confusion. He ignores it, necking the glass of golden bubbly liquid before descending the steps and wrapping a hand around my waist.

"Don't. People will ask questions," I hiss.

He smiles at someone over my shoulder. "No, they won't. I want them to see. Now smile." I smile at him.

"I need to get out of here," I say through clenched teeth.

He pulls me close, wrapping his arms tightly around my waist. "Touch me," he demands when my arms remain rigid at my sides. Complying with his request, I slide one palm up his chest, and the other around the back of his neck. His mouth drops to my neck, but he never makes contact. "They won't let guests leave until I say so." And he can't clear it too soon as he needs to avoid suspicion. "Dance with me. Act like you want me." I can hear the smile in his voice and it has me wanting to kidney punch him.

"I'd rather cut you," I say, smiling sweetly.

He takes my hand and a strange tingle buzzes up my arm, almost like electricity humming over my skin. I frown down at our intertwined fingers. He leads me to the small clearance in the middle of the patio where a string quartet are seated and playing the kind of music that Nicholai listens to.

He spins me and I pivot on my toe. I can dance. Dancing and fighting are one and the same, a pattern, the meeting of bodies, a liaison in which you must read your partner and either follow them or counter them. His hand presses into the small of my back, wrenching me against his hard body so abruptly that I lose my breath on a gasp. His full lips curve on one side and that shadow of a dimple sinks into his stubble-covered cheek. I follow every movement he lays down. Our bodies moving together like hot and cold water, fluid, different and yet exactly the same.

"I'm impressed," he rumbles against my ear.

"I'm offended," I reply. He huffs a low laugh and his warm breath blows against the skin of my throat. "Nero, I really need to get out of here."

He pulls back and looks in my eyes, his expression so hard, so resolved that he looks as though he would tear down entire countries in this moment. "I won't let anything happen to you." His hold on me tightens, and I suddenly realize that I don't mind. Any touch is enough to make me want to kill, but...silence. The pounding need is just absent.

"I'm a big girl." Swallowing down the feeling of unease in my gut, I attempt to brush off his comment.

"You are, Morte." He spins me again, his grip firm and unrelenting as he moves me across the dance floor.

The worrying thing is that I believe him. I trust him when he says he'll protect me, even though I don't need his protection. Nero Verdi is the most dangerous man I've ever encountered, and yet, there's something about him. I can't put my finger on it, but I'm certainly not as guarded as I should be around a man like him. He throws me off and it's unsettling. After all, complacency will get you killed. I know that all too well.

NERO

S he relaxes in my arms and her fingers tighten, clinging to my bicep. When I walked into that room she was hovering over my brother like a beautiful avenger, a walking angel of death bearing down on her victim with the strangest expression, somewhere between blissful relief and anguish. The way she moves, the way she looks at me even now is that of a predator, a killer, a demon in a dress, and I'd be lying if I said she doesn't make my blood heat.

I glance over her head and see two guards jog up to a couple more on the gate, speaking into radios. I told them to handle it, whilst assuring them that I should go back to the party to give the illusion of normalcy. Of course, the guests will be told what actually happened, but right now, revealing the truth will not only incite panic but also look weak. The fact that the Italian Mafia sustained a hit within their own walls at an engagement party...well, that's just embarrassing, but Arnaldo planned for this. And really, if the truth comes out, Lorenzo will look like the weak one, killed because he was trying to fuck another woman at his own engagement party. I can't help but smile. His father would be rolling in his grave. But it's this very fact that will keep this entire thing quiet. People might whisper that it was my date who killed him, but no one will ever confirm it. Other than his direct security, I guarantee no one will ever know. Reputation means far more than justice in our world.

"They're searching the guests," Una breathes against my throat, her voice strained. I spin her, switching our positions. Sure enough, the guards are looking at the guests, searching bags, and I'm sure looking for a mysterious brunette. I doubt they'll look at Una, but they might. After all, she technically never came through the gate. If they check, we're fucked.

I spin her again and smile, hoping we look like the perfect couple. Keeping my eyes trained on the approaching guards, I watch them draw closer. The people around us start to slow, paying more attention to the guards as they fan out into the dancers. A flash of panic crosses Una's eyes, and I worry that she'll do something rash, like turn this party into a bloodbath.

"Sir," someone says behind me.

Shit. I grab the back of Una's neck and wrench her to me, slamming my lips over hers. She freezes, her nails digging into my shoulder. Trailing my hand down her back, I brush her ass as I caress my tongue over her bottom lip. This needs to look good, good enough to make people uncomfortable. She stiffens and tries to shove away from me, putting up a fight. Damn it. Right now, our fates are intertwined. If she gets caught then so do I.

Taking control, I thrust my hand into her hair and grab a handful of it, pulling the strands roughly. The second I do, she releases a sharp breath. her lips part, and breath dancing over my tongue. The ice cracks inch by inch until she's soft and pliant in my arms. Her fingers trail from my shoulder to the back of my neck, nails raking over my skin in a burning trail that has me hissing against her lips and pulling her tighter against my body. She tastes of champagne and danger, and everything about her has adrenaline slamming through my veins like a drug. The kiss becomes a battleground, the rougher I am, the more bruising my grip, the deeper she falls. There's nothing sweet or gentle in it, just brutal passion. She bites my lip hard enough to draw blood, and then swipes her tongue over the wound, making me groan. My cock is plastered against my zipper and heat rips over my skin in a wave. Finally releasing my grip on her hair, she staggers away from me, gasping for breath. Her wide eyes meet mine, those lilac-tinged irises swirling with confusion and lust. She looks horrified.

We stand in a sea of people, but all I feel is her. My skin prickles and I grit my jaw as need and desire pulse through my veins. Una is a tool, an assassin, the enemy. Anything. She is anything but what I'm seeing her as right now – someone I want to sink balls deep inside. The personal and the professional must always be kept separate in this business, especially when you're dealing with the kiss of death. Squeezing my eyes shut for a few seconds, I take a deep breath before turning and walking away from her. That kiss saved us, for now. I need to get us out of here.

I approach Romero, Lorenzo's second. He folds his arms over his chest and squares his shoulders, glaring at me in a way that promises retribution. To the outside world, Lorenzo and I were brothers. Only Lorenzo and I, along with our closest friends, knew the truth. We were bitter enemies, and I just won.

"We need to start moving guests out of here."

Jet-black eyebrows drop over equally dark eyes as he

assesses me. "I'm going to kill you," he growls. I smile, noticing the vein at his temple throb.

I huff a laugh. "Would that you could. Your fearless leader is dead, Romero. Who do you think will take his place?"

He snarls, getting in my face. "You're a bastard. The family will never back you."

I laugh. "You're right, I am a bastard."

I bask in the knowledge that Lorenzo – my father's first born, his heir, his son, his greatest accomplishment – was fucking weak. And I, the unwanted bastard son, the result of my mother's infidelity, have won. I'd truly hate him if I weren't actually grateful. You see, Lorenzo had his love, and it did him no favours. No, Matteo Santos forged me. His hatred made me strong. His constant reminders of what I am made me smart. His physical blows made me a fighter. I learned from him that respect and power are not a birth right. He had the power of his name, but no matter how many times he beat me, I never felt an ounce of respect towards him. My sole purpose is to destroy his empire, piece by piece. I killed him, and now his son is gone. Sometimes, I wish I'd stayed my hand, so he could have been here to watch his son fall, so he could have died knowing that I would take over. I am a bastard, but it means nothing because I will take everything and more.

"Move the fucking guests out. Now," I growl.

Romero clenches his jaw, the muscles in his shoulders tightening dangerously. I want him to, I really do. Instead, he turns and walks away. A few minutes later the guests start to leave, and I don't see Una again. She disappeared like an apparition, a ghost on the wind.

5

UNA

I'm striding down a hotel stairwell, trying to look inconspicuous as I make my way to the underground parking deck. With my blood-stained dress and semi-automatic rifle, the elevator wasn't exactly an option. My phone rings just as I reach the underground level and I touch my earpiece.

"Not a good time," I growl.

"I've been trying to get a hold of you for the last week. So tell me, when is a good time?"

Nero.

"I've been off the grid."

"No shit."

There's something about him that manages to elicit a certain level of irritation, dare I say, anger. It's a skill; really it is, because I don't do angry. Anger is a useless emotion and only serves to blind reason.

"Look, is there a reason for this call?" I pant.

"Of course. I have a job for you."

"Have Arnie contact me."

He huffs a laugh. "Oh, Una. I think we're past that."

Really? This guy. "I don't," I say bluntly. The door at the top of the stairs crashes open, the sound echoing around the empty concrete stairwell. "Shit!" I have a good lead but I'd still rather get out clean. Someone fires a couple of rounds and they ping off the metal bannister next to me.

"You sound busy." I can hear the amusement in his voice.

"No shit," I growl, shoving through the door. "Text me a location. I'll be there tomorrow." I hang up and pick up the pace, sprinting across the parking deck. I jump in the Porsche parked under a broken light and slam my hand over the start button. The engine purrs to life and I ram my foot on the accelerator, making it spit and snarl as the tires shriek against the tarmac.

Leng's men burst onto the street just as I pull away from the hotel. That was close. Too close.

Pressing speed dial, I listen to the earpiece ring out with a dial tone. "Una." Olov answers on the first ring.

"I'm twenty minutes away. Be ready to leave immediately," I tell him, speaking in quick-fire Russian. He hangs up and I speed towards the private airfield on the outskirts of Singapore.

6

NERO

F lipping open the top of my cigarette packet, I take one out, placing it between my lips. I sit behind the very desk my father used to, the desk Lorenzo sat at until just two weeks ago. I'm the capo of New York. These are dangerous times though. I'm keeping my inner circle tight, only dealing directly with the three guys in this room. Jackson is pacing in front of my desk, clenching and releasing his fists repeatedly. Gio is leaning against the far wall with his arms crossed over his chest and a scowl fixed on his face. Tommy's sitting on one of the sofas, a drink in one hand and a cigarette in the other as he stares blankly at the opposite wall. His sleeves are rolled up, his forearms and the material of his white shirt painted in blood. The tell-tale splatter of a slit throat sprayed across his neck. He and Jackson were involved in a deal that went south earlier tonight, and one of his guys was taken out. It got messy. It was expected though. Any takeover will be met with a certain amount of resistance. People think they can move the goal posts, demand new terms, more territory, better prices. It's my job to make it clear that the only one who

will be renegotiating here is me. Power is all about perception and fear. If I have to paint the streets with their blood
to get my point across, I will.

"We should go back there and kill every fucking one of
them." Jackson's gaze meets mine, every muscle tense with
the need for retribution. He's a big guy, broad-shouldered
and lethal if you're on his bad side. I lean back in my chair
as I lift the lighter to my face. The heavy click of the silver
zippo is the only sound in the room aside from his ragged
breaths. I inhale, drawing the smoke into my lungs, letting
it fill me, burning me from the inside out.

"No."

"Fuck!" he shouts, pushing away from the desk. "Levi
is dead because of those motherfuckers!" I still, tilting my
head to the side as I look up at him. He stares back at me
for a long moment before swallowing nervously. I push up
from the desk and slowly move around it. Everyone in the
room seems to hold their breath. I stop only when I'm
standing nose to nose with him. There's a pause, a tense
moment where we just stare each other down. He's like a
brother to me, but brother or not, no one questions me.

"You don't get to think, Jackson. You don't get an opin-
ion," I growl under my breath. A muscle in his jaw ticks
and it's enough to piss me off. Slamming a hand around
his throat, I squeeze hard enough to make him choke.
"You are a fucking soldier! Get out." Releasing him, he
staggers away from me, heading straight for the door.

He pauses when a loud click sounds behind me,
turning around with his hand already reaching for his gun.
Gio moves away from the wall, gun already trained on the
glass French doors that lead to the balcony. I turn around,
squinting to see into the darkness on the other side of the
glass. I can just make out someone in black, crouched
down. The handle is twisted and the tiny figure waltzes

into the room like she owns the place. A black hood hides half her face, but I'd know those red painted lips anywhere.

"Boys." Una smiles and then in the blink of an eye her gun is pointing at me, one bright red fingertip lingering over the trigger. She lifts her head enough that I can just make her eyes out. "Nero. Power looks good on you." She winks. "Send them out," she orders, jerking her head towards the three guys, two of which have weapons trained on her.

You could cut the tension in the room with a knife, that is until Tommy laughs. "I like her," he mumbles around his cigarette, as though she didn't have a loaded gun pointed at me, and absolutely no conscience to stop her from pulling the trigger.

I step forward, closing the distance between us. "Sociable as ever, I see."

Her smile widens and she cocks a brow. I'm pretty sure she's not going to shoot me, but truthfully, I can't predict what she'll do because she plays by her own set of rules.

"I don't play well with others," she says, a little pout forming on her lips. I keep closing in on her until the barrel of her gun presses against my forehead.

"You're not going to shoot me. A capo is worth, what? A couple of million?" Her head tilts, eyes tracing over me predatorily. "You don't work for free." I smirk.

Her eyes dance dangerously and she trails the gun from my forehead down over my temple. Her scent assaults me – vanilla and just a hint of gun oil. She glides the cool metal over my cheek and along my jaw. That tight body of hers is so close I can feel every breath she takes as her tits press against my stomach. That ruthless look is in her eye, the same one she wore after she killed my brother. That look, the gun on my cheek… it makes my dick hard. I have to bite back a groan when she leans in, brushing her lips over my jaw until she reaches my ear.

"Send. Them. Out," she purrs, ramming the gun underneath my chin hard enough to force my head back.

The barrel bites into my skin and a low laugh works its way up my throat. It's only when you're staring death in the face that you truly remember you're alive. My blood rushes through my veins, forcing adrenaline through my body. Smiling, I click my fingers, gesturing for them to get out. Tommy gets up and leaves without a backwards glance. That fucker doesn't give a shit. Jackson moves next, and Gio is the last, ever loyal, and far too serious.

"You can't put me down before I put him down," Una drawls, sounding almost bored, reading him without even sparing him a glance.

"Go, Gio." Maybe I should be more worried about her, but she's not going to shoot me. I know she's not.

He sighs and steps out of the room, closing the door behind him. I have no doubt he's lingering just on the other side. She clicks the safety on and holsters her gun at her hip before stepping back very deliberately. I drop into the chair behind my desk. For a long while she simply stands, surveying every inch of the room.

"So, you kept the ugly house."

"A show of power." I hate this house, but to the family here in New York, this is the capo's house. To reside in it is symbolic of the power I now hold. I don't give a shit. I'd happily burn it to the ground with them all in it.

She approaches my desk and takes a seat in front of me, making a slow show of crossing one leg over the other as she trails one blood-red nail over her thigh. She pulls her hood back and the light touches her fully for the first time since she walked in here. Hers is a cold beauty, almost inhuman, because set into the youthful face of an angel is the hard severity of someone who has seen and done unspeakable things. There's an argument for everything, and I won't pretend I'm any better. I've done things that would make even the hardest of men flinch, but they were done in the name of something. Power, family, more power...take your pick. What Una does though...she fights for no one, not even herself. Let's see if I can change that.

"I have a job for you."

She laughs quietly. "I came here as a courtesy, Nero." She takes a knife out of a thigh holster and casually flips it through her fingers. "You helped me once. But you do not summon me. You do not hire me." She slams the knife in the antique wooden desk hard enough that her knuckles turn white around the hilt. "You are a capo," she spits, those violet eyes locking with mine.

I sigh. The problem with Una...she's the top of the food chain and she swims with sharks. She hasn't realised yet, I am a motherfucking shark, circling in the dark waters right beneath them all, waiting, biding my time. I explode out of my chair and have my hand around her throat in a heartbeat, slamming her down on the desk.

"You make the mistake of thinking that mere titles mean anything to me. I get what I want, and what I want right now, Morte, is you," I growl at her. A wide grin stretches her lips. It's the first time I've seen her genuinely smile.

"Nero, you say the hottest things." She shifts and wraps her legs around my waist. I cock a brow at her and then she locks her ankles together, tightening her thighs around me like a boa constrictor. When I readjust my grip on her throat, she bites her lip, as if she likes it. Her hips shift, and I bite back a groan as she yanks me even closer, squeezing me into the gap between her thighs. She narrows her eyes and her body trembles with the effort of trying to hurt me.

My kidneys are screaming in protest, but my dick is begging to be inside her. I have a kamikaze cock. Her hips rock, the friction forcing a low growl from my throat. I pull her up from the desk by her throat, holding her only inches away from me.

"You are disposable to me, Una," I breathe. Her lips part, drawing my eyes to them, so full and perfect. I feel her strangled breaths on my face, her rapid heartbeat beneath my fingertips and most of all, I feel her pussy pressing against my cock. She laughs, breath wheezing past her lips. I fight with my own control as I walk the fine line between wanting to fuck her and strangle her. We remain locked together like that for a few seconds, and it's torture. Shit! I don't have time for this. Finally, I release her and push away from her body. Her legs unwind from around me and she coughs, sitting up and clutching at her throat.

"You have a firm grip."

I walk to the wall, bracing my forearm against it. I need her. I can't kill her, and as for fucking her…they don't call her the 'kiss of death' for nothing. Apparently, my dick didn't get the memo.

"I don't have time for this bullshit, Una!"

She lets out a tinkling laugh, so at odds with the killer she is. "I like you, Nero." I turn to face her, watching as she crosses her legs on the desk. "I respect you, and you've moved up in the world." She gestures to the room around us, the very room in which she killed Lorenzo. "But not enough that I work for you. There's an order, a balance. You may not care for titles, but the world does. You may think I'm disposable, but let me assure you, there's only one Una Ivanov and my services are very much in demand."

"I'll pay you."

She smiles and drags her hand through her long blonde hair. "You couldn't afford me."

Taking a deep breath, I reach for the packet of cigarettes inside my pocket. I watch her tense, and suddenly, the blade she impaled in my desk is in her hand. I narrow my eyes. "If I wanted you dead, you'd be dead." I repeat the words she once said to me as I pull the cigarettes out.

She drops onto her feet, pulling her hood up and making her way towards the doors she came in through. "See you around, *capo*."

I take the unlit cigarette from my mouth and hold it, pausing. This is it, the pivotal moment where all my plans will either succeed or fail, because without her, it all falls to shit. "I know where your sister is." She freezes, and I put the cigarette back in my mouth, lighting it. By the time I take my first drag, she still hasn't turned around. I wait, watching the rapid rise and fall of her shoulders.

"I don't have a sister." Her voice is like thunder, rolling, building.

I fight a smile. I have her. "Anna Vasiliev, born March 6 1991."

Whipping around to face me, I see the indecision written all over her face, the confusion, the fracture. The cool calm and sheer indifference that make up Una Ivanov, crack and splinter. She might as well have exposed her jugular to me. Getting what you want from people is easy, you just have to find their weakness. I'll admit, finding hers was difficult, until I had someone go to Russia and start digging. I've had to pay more money for information on her than I think I would have for the president. Of course, Una Ivanov isn't her real name. Nicholai Ivanov, boss of the Russian Bratva, gave her that name. He thinks of Una as his daughter, and named her so. The woman has powerful allies; I'll give her that. Her real name, Una

Vasiliev. An orphan. Until she disappeared at age thirteen that is. I guess not many people would go out of their way to find an orphan. For the most part, she's a ghost.

I look in her eyes and see it, a spark, hope. She wants to believe me. She wants what I say to be true. I see the divide, the fight within her. Hope versus the rational, smart decision, because hope without reason is such a frail, weak emotion. But weakness is a part of human nature. Una barely seems human, always professional, measured, deadly. Will she be rational now, or will she find a slither of humanity? Heart or head? That is the question.

7

UNA

My heart is hammering, the pulse in my throat pounding so hard I can barely breathe. Nero takes a slow drag of his cigarette, watching me like a hawk, looking for any sign of weakness. Little does he know, he might as well have liver punched me, because I feel paralysed right now. How does he know about Anna? No one knows about the sister I was torn away from when the bratva took me from an orphanage thirteen years ago. I spent years being trained, beaten, broken, only to be rebuilt into the embodiment of the perfect soldier. The bratva made me strong, they made me a warrior, they made me exactly what they wanted. Una Vasiliev died in that place, everything that she was stripped from her. Except Anna, because I could never let her go, even when I wanted to, even when I knew my obsession with her brought me nothing but pain and unanswered questions.

I never mention her, and my silent search for her is my own. Finding Anna is near impossible. All the answers lie within the bratva, a place in which I have status and privilege, but if Nicholai realized I had a weakness, he'd search for her and kill her himself. And he'd genuinely believe he was doing me a favour, setting me free. Maybe he would be, but when I think of my sister, my innocent, sweet sister, a deep ache buries itself into my chest. Anna was never strong. She was sweet and good, and she depended on me. I shielded her innocent eyes from the ugliness of the world, corrupted myself, sold my soul off piece by piece, and I did it willingly, to keep her safe, to keep her pure. And that was just in the orphanage. My greatest failing in life is the inability to protect her. But now I can...if I could find her.

Do I believe Nero? I don't know. But just hearing her name fall from his lips has something inside of me shifting. A door that I firmly slammed shut when I was fifteen years old is now open a crack. Emotions are seeping out and I'm fighting to shove them back into that dark corner of my mind where Una Vasiliev lives, the young girl crying for her sister, hurting for all that she lost, for all that she had to do to survive. I feel. For the first time in a very long time, I feel something besides the cold detachment that comes with killing. I'd forgotten what anger feels like...to be so consumed, so utterly driven by that sole emotion. I'm angry at myself, but mostly I'm angry at Nero for using her against me, for cornering me, despite the fact that I know I would do far worse to get what I want. I feel threatened, and that's never good. Rolling my shoulders and closing my eyes, the icy rage locks around me, imprisoning me in its grasp. And the switch flips. I have no more control over it than the instinct to draw breath. When I open my eyes, my senses have sharpened, my vision becomes clearer, and I can sense every single breath he takes. Adrenaline courses through my veins. My mind perceives a threat, and my body is responding automatically. After years of training, it's no more than a reflex, like someone throwing you a ball and your arm moving to catch it. I'm ready to fight. Ready to kill.

"You found a name. Well done," I say. Even to my own ears I sound cold, efficient. Nero raises a brow. His eyes lock with mine and I see wariness there, but not fear, never fear from him. Silly. "What did you think, Nero? That you'd dig up a name and have me doing your dirty work like some pet?" A smile pulls at my lips. "I've been very nice to you until now, I really have, but do not lie to me. Do not piss me off. I will end you and never think of you again," I whisper.

His expression remains impassive, almost bored. Something in me delights in his unspoken challenge. He stands there, authority and power pouring off him in waves. The dark lord on the mafia throne. "I'm not lying. And you could kill me, but then you'd never know, would you?" Those deep brown eyes hold my gaze, and doubt starts to take hold of me.

What if he's telling the truth? Or maybe I just want to believe him. I hate that this is even a subject of discussion. I should just walk away now. I haven't seen Anna in over thirteen years; she should be nothing more than a ghost to me..

"This isn't a trap, Una. This is a simple exchange of favours," he says, his voice deep and melodic.

I move to the desk, bracing my hands against it with my back to him. "Fucking mafia with your favours." I don't like this. I'm untouchable, but right now I feel like I've torn open my own ribcage and am daring him to thrust a blade into my beating heart.

I glance over my shoulder. "What do you want?" I ask, and he smiles, blowing a long stream of smoke through his lips. I'm the starving lion lingering just outside the confines of a trap. Nero is dangling Anna in front of me like a piece of prime rib, and he knows I'm going to walk inside. I can't resist. I guess we all have our weaknesses, even me.

"Simple. You help me destroy my enemies."

Simple, he says. I know all about his antics in the last two weeks since I killed Lorenzo. Turns out, Nero is the bad boy of the mafia, and considering it's the damn mafia, that's saying something. Arnaldo appointed him capo in the wake of his brother's death, and now shit is hitting the fan. The Italians value family and honour above all else. Turns out Nero values neither. He's a ruthless fuck, but then I already knew that. I had him pegged the moment I met him. Still, decapitating Lorenzo's second was extreme and probably isn't in the team building and leadership manual. Nero Verdi has enemies coming out of his asshole. I have no desire to share them with him.

Turning to face him, I square my shoulders and tilt my head to the side. "I hear you have many enemies, *Capo*. What with killing your own brother for the throne." I tsk. "Nasty business, especially when you Italians value family so much."

A twisted smile pulls at his lips and smoke drifts around his face; rising and making him look like the devil himself. "Ah, but the question is, how much do you value *your* family, *Morte*?" He emphasises the word, purring it as though it were an endearment.

I grit my teeth. "What's the job?"

He approaches and pulls a piece of paper from the inside pocket of his jacket, holding it out to me. I take it from him, and he drops into the chair behind his desk. Unfolding the sheet of lined paper, I find four names scrawled one below the other.

Marco Fiore

Bernardo Caro

Franco Lama

Finnegan O'Hara

I recognise three of them and two of them are no street rats. Bernardo Caro is another New York capo, and Finnegan O'Hara...well, he's into everything and everyone. There are several hits on his head. I'm already thinking of my contacts, how I could get to them, who I should hit first... I slowly lift my eyes to him. He's watching me, one elbow resting on his desk and his index finger tapping over his bottom lip. I fold the paper and hand it back.

"I can't hit this many in one network." Three of those guys are Italian. It would draw too much attention, and in this business, attention is never good.

He shrugs, pursing his lips around his cigarette as he inhales. The end glows a bright cherry red and he flashes me a dark look. "Then good luck finding your sister." Smoke drifts between his lips as he speaks.

I clench my fists so hard that my nails break the skin on my palm. "You don't understand," I growl. "The way I work, I maintain a fine balance. I'm unbiased in my services, and therefore I have somewhat of a diplomatic immunity among the crime organizations. If I do this for you, I'm not leaving my name on it. It's bad for business." Not to mention that if someone decides I'm a threat or that I'm taking sides, it'll be open season on my head. I'll have no choice but to go back to Russia for protection, and I may never find Anna.

He shakes his head. "I need them to know it was you and not me."

"Does it matter? Someone has to hire me."

He smirks. "Plausible deniability."

This is suicide, but it's amazing what you'll do for the thing you want most. I've spent my entire life alone, an island surrounded by waters so deep and dark, no one could ever hope to cross them. But Anna...she walks on water. My boundaries don't apply to her, or the fantasy of her at least. Who knows who or what she's become now. "If I agree to this, it will take time," I say reluctantly.

"I've got time." His lips kick up at one side. "I'll pay you three for each one. Plus your sister. You work no other jobs until this is complete and you stay with me."

Jeez, I guess he's wealthier than I thought. Wait, what?

I tilt my head, narrowing my eyes. "Yeah, that's not going to happen. I'm not good with people."

He smirks. "No people, just me. I have a penthouse in the city."

I glare at him. "Why? I have an apartment in the city. Surely you know my sister is enough incentive for you to trust me."

He moves back to his desk, stubbing out his cigarette in the steel ashtray. His head remains tilted down as he flicks the butt away. "My reasons are my own. Take it or leave it."

Why would he want me in his house? That's where he's most vulnerable.

"I'll agree if you can give me proof." I swallow hard, trying hard to hide just how much this means. "I want proof that you have something on Anna."

"So you can find her yourself and sell me out?" We stare at each other for long moments, those whisky eyes of his, so hard, so calculating. Finally, he pushes his chair back and pulls open the bottom drawer. He takes out a photograph, holding it against his chest until I look up and meet his gaze. "If you betray me, if you cut and run, I will send this photograph to Nicholai Ivanov," he says coldly.

My expression must give away my fury, because he places the picture on the desk. Ignoring him, I rush forward to look at the photo. It's blurry and distorted; the image zoomed in from a distance. It's dark, but there's a line of girls, all of them bound at the wrists. Two men stand with guns, on either side of the women. In the middle of the image is a girl. She can be no older than eighteen. Her white-blonde hair hangs over her face, and I can barely make out her profile, but it's a face I would know anywhere. Anna.

"Where did you get this?" I whisper.

"This was taken three years ago in Juarez. A shipment of slaves were sold to the Sinaloa Cartel."

My blood runs cold and it feels like someone has wrapped a fist around my heart. "A slave? In the cartel?"

His lips press into a flat line. He says nothing, but his silence is answer enough. My fingers tighten on the edge of the desk, and I feel. I feel…everything. Emotion bubbles up my throat, and I bite hard on the inside of my cheek in an attempt to channel it, but I can't. My long dormant heart feels like it's breaking, splintering open and bleeding out. My mind flashes through memories, only instead of seeing them as myself, I imagine it's her. Men holding her down, laughing as they tear her clothing from her body, hands clamping around her delicate throat, nails raking over soft skin as they force her legs apart. Only she wouldn't fight like I did, and she wouldn't have a Nicholai to save her. My nails scream in protest as I grip the wood hard enough to bend them back. White-hot rage rips over my skin, and I want nothing more than to make the rivers of Mexico run red until I find her. Images blink behind my eyelids like a faulty film reel, and it makes me want to scream.

"Una!" Fingers brush over my jaw, and I flinch back as Nero tears me from the screaming in my mind. "Look at me." My heart is hammering, and I can feel the thin layer of sweat coating my skin. "Una, look at me." He repeats.

Hands land on either side of my face, his grip strong and deliberate, forcing me to lift my eyes.

Meeting Nero's gaze, his perceptive eyes search mine. I'm frozen, stuck in a place between the past and the present, reality and nightmare. His thumb strokes over my cheek and it's like breaking the surface after being submerged in water for several minutes. I drag in a staggered breath, sucking the oxygen into my lungs. My focus snaps back into place almost instantly and I slam my palm against his chest with enough force that he moves back a step, his hands falling away from me. Backing up, I begin pacing around the desk, putting distance between us. Of all the people to have a relapse in front of...

"Do we have a deal?" His expression shutters once again.

My jaw hurts from gritting my teeth so hard. "I'll kill your people, but I want more than just your information on Anna." He lifts his chin. "I want you to help me get her back." It's a small price to pay. For her.

Whatever his plan, it must be important because he nods quickly. "Done." He puts the photo back in the drawer and slides it shut. "I have to handle something, and then I'll take you home." Great. I'd almost forgotten that I'm going to have to live with him.

———

FIFTEEN MINUTES PASS, and when Nero doesn't come back I get annoyed and bored. I'm not some staff member he can just keep at his beck and call. Screw this. I leave the office and make my way through the house, ducking into doorways whenever I see any of his men. I manage to make it into the sunroom where I slip outside unnoticed. Making my way across the sloping lawns, I inhale the cool night air, allowing it to help calm my racing mind.

When I'm away from the house, I call Sasha. "Hello," he answers in Russian. I smile. Sasha is one of the few people I trust in this world. We grew up together, were trained together and shaped into what we now are. He's as close to a brother as I will ever get.

"Sasha, it's me." I slip easily into my native tongue, although it feels strangely foreign. I've been away for so long now.

"Una. Where are you?"

"On a job in New York." I don't say more than that and he doesn't ask. This is our life, this is what we do. Although, he'd be disappointed if he knew I was selling myself out right now, not to mention he'd tell Nicholai. I went to Nicholai's facility when I was thirteen after he saved me from being raped and sold as a whore. Sasha was there from the age of nine. I'm loyal to Nicholai because he's the only father I've ever known, but I see his flaws. He would kill Anna, and I know he would do it because he loves me. In many ways, I see his logic, I even agree with it. I just can't allow it, not when it's Anna. Sasha, on the other hand, has complete loyalty to Nicholai. He has no weakness such as a long-lost sister. I care for him like a brother and he cares for me too, but ultimately, he would betray me before he would breach Nicholai's trust. I have to be careful. "I need a favour."

"Oh?"

"But you have to promise me you won't breathe a word of this to anyone." The pleading tone in my voice is pathetic really.

"Fine," he says, reluctantly.

"I need you to locate where the Sinaloa Cartel keep their sex slaves."

He goes silent. "You do realise they keep thousands of slaves?"

I sigh and pinch the bridge of my nose.

"Are you looking for someone specific?"

"Yes."

He says nothing for long seconds and then releases a long breath. "Well, are you going to tell me who?"

"She won't be under the same name now. You're looking for a girl sold into the Sinaloa about three years ago. White-blonde hair, blue eyes."

He clears his throat. "Okay, I can't promise anything, but I'll have a look." The other thing Sasha specializes in is hacking. The dark web, bank accounts, emails, even CCTV footage. If there is a trace of Anna to be found, he'll find it. I admit, it's a long shot.

"Thank you." I hang up and drag a hand through my hair. We now live in an online world, and even the criminals have moved into a new era. Weapons dealers, sex traffickers, drug dealers...you can buy rocket launchers on the dark web. Gun traffickers have their own version of eBay. Just as they always have done, they have a dark and sordid underground, even within our own Internet. It's here that Sasha and I often find our prey. Don't mistake us for some kind of good Samaritan's though. We take them out for someone else who probably wants to take their place or whose own illicit trade is threatened. That's the way the world keeps turning, with those who have power garnering more on the backs of someone else. People like Anna are sold and traded like cattle, and for the most part, no one can touch the men who do it. Every so often though, someone like me crawls out of the woodwork. In many ways, I've been equally robbed of my life, but I have a purpose. When I find Anna, and I will find her one way or another, I'm going to slaughter anyone who had a hand in taking her.

Nero may know roughly where Anna is but I'm not about to sit back and let him take his sweet time in finding her, just so he can get what he wants from me. I'm no one's pawn. I need more information though. If Sasha can't find anything, then I'm left with Nero as my only hope of ever finding her. That doesn't sit well. I want to kill him and smile as I watch him bleed out, but I can't and I won't. He found Anna. Despite the unlimited resources at my disposal and a reputation that tends to make people talk, I couldn't find her. He succeeded where I failed. How? I've looked, but I guess I never really thought I would find her, and now that I'm faced with the possibility, now that I've seen her, she's suddenly more than just a fading memory.

My thoughts are interrupted when I hear footsteps brushing over the grass. The distraction is a welcome reprieve from my thoughts, and part of me hopes it's an attacker. I need a fight right now. I need the violence and bloodshed to remind me what I am. Listening, I blow out a breath that fogs around my face. Despite the days being warm in April, the nights are still cold here in New York. Of course, compared to Russia it's positively sweltering. I don't miss those freezing cold winters in that concrete fortress.

Turning as the footsteps get closer, I see one of Nero's guys approaching, the quiet one. His black suit blends into the darkness as though he were a part of it. His eyes scan the night as he approaches me, as though looking for any hidden threats. I keep my face tilted down, shielding it from his view.

"I'm Gio, Nero's second," he says, his voice a little too cultured for New York. He has all the traditional Italian features except for his deep blue eyes, and he's almost as handsome as Nero, but he lacks that ruthless edge that makes the capo more somehow.

"Does that mean I'm supposed to trust you?"

A humorless smirk cuts over his face. "It means he has my loyalty. And for now, so do you."

"You know I'm a threat to him."

"Nero doesn't need my protection. Trust me." I believe him. "Why are you out here?"

On a sigh, I scoop my hood off my face. He's Nero's second. I can't hide my face from him for the extended period of time this job is likely to take. "I'm not running if that's what you're worried about. I made a deal."

"A deal you're not happy with," he counters.

I tilt my head to the side and smirk. "Whatever gave you that idea?" I startle when two black shapes come barrelling down the sloped gardens towards us. My muscles tense but Gio doesn't move. When they're a few feet away I see they're dogs. Two black Dobermans circle his legs excitedly until he barks a command at them and they drop to a sit, one on each side.

"Nice dogs," I remark, watching the way they study me intently.

"They're Nero's. This is Zeus." He places his hand on the one on his right. "And George." He points to the one on the left. It's George who breaks his vigil, as though he can't contain himself. He jumps up and rushes towards me, his ears back and his little stump of a tail wagging. Smiling, I lean over and run my hands over his slick, black coat. "Real smooth, George," Gio huffs. "Some guard dog you are." Zeus stays where he is while George leans against my legs, begging me for attention.

"He called his dog George?" I look up at him, cocking a brow.

He shrugs. "Come on. I'll show you around."

I glance back at the ugly house sitting just above us on the hill. "I'm good. Where's Nero?"

"He's unexpectedly pre-occupied."

"Okay, either you take me to him or I'm leaving. And you can tell him that I don't wait around for anyone."

He turns and starts walking towards the house with a low chuckle. "This is going to be good."

Falling in beside him, we walk in silence. The smell of night lilies assaults me as we pass through the gardens. Roses adorn the flowerbeds, their crimson petals bleeding against the night. The dogs break away, running ahead of us into the sunroom at the back of the house. I pull my hood up as we enter. It makes me uneasy being around all these people, being seen. Gio leads me along a corridor until we come to a door that opens onto a set of concrete stairs. A burst of cool air drift up them as we descend into the basement, like icy fingers, reaching for us. At the bottom, he approaches an old, rusted metal door, then presses a code into a keypad, eliciting a loud click. With a rough shove he pushes the old door open, its hinges screaming in protest.

"Here you go." He stands back, gesturing me to move ahead of him. I don't like it, but I steel my spine and step inside, keeping my focus on him. Gio is the worst kind of dangerous. The first impression is that he's nice, intelligent, smiles easily and has an air of kindness to him. Everything about him makes you forget that he would put a bullet in your head quick as look at you if the situation called for it. I don't forget though. He didn't make it to Nero's second by being soft.

As I step through the door, a gruesome scene unfolds before me. The room is nothing more than a large, empty space with concrete walls and floor. A drain is set into the middle of the floor, which gently slopes in towards it. The entire room smells of blood and death, and the floor is stained with evidence of the acts committed within these walls. It reminds me of the facility I grew up in, concrete and blood. Directly above the drain is a body, suspended by the ankles via thick metal chains that hang from a hook in the ceiling. The man is barely more than pulverised flesh, his face completely unrecognisable. The big guy that was in Nero's office earlier stands in front of him, his shirt-sleeves rolled up and a set of brass knuckles clutched in his hand. Blood coats his fingers, spreading up his forearms and catching the edge of his shirtsleeves. Nero and the other guy that were in the office are off to the side. Nero leans against the wall, a cigarette hanging between his lips. He almost seems casual, but I know better.

"This is Tommy." Gio points to the guy straddling a chair right next to Nero and he lifts a hand, waving at me as he grins. He's the only one here who doesn't have the dark hair and olive skin. His green eyes, pale skin and chestnut hair give him away as something other than Italian. "And Jackson." He waves a hand dismissively towards the big guy. This is Nero's inner circle, I realise. Every capo, boss or leader has one. You have to. I have people I use for certain things. No one can stand completely alone. It's impossible.

Sighing, I move over to the wall where Nero's standing, prepared to watch them flex their muscles and treat the guy on the chain like a piñata. Nero's arm is a couple of feet away from mine where I brace against the cold concrete, but I'm abnormally aware of him. He stands in his silent vigil, king of all he surveys, and it's everything that he doesn't say or do that makes him so formidable. Nicholai always said that a man's weight is all in how he is perceived, and perception can always be altered. A man who makes threats, a man who is seen to commit violence is doing so because he feels he has to make a point. Nero wants me to take out his enemies. He's not making a point, far from it, he's deliberately trying to remove himself from it. He doesn't need to make threats or kill people, because he knows what he is and he's confident in his abilities. I can feel his eyes on my face but I ignore it, crossing my arms over my chest as I school my features into a bored expression. Truthfully, once you've seen one interrogation, you've seen them all.

Gio approaches the suspended man, circling him with his hands buried deep in his pockets. "Is he dead?"

Jackson cracks his neck to the side impatiently. He's the muscle, the most reckless of the three, the most easily riled or baited, I note. "It can be arranged."

"If we wanted him dead, I'd have used a bullet and saved your shirt," Gio lilts, his voice like velvet as he says the words quietly. "Wake him up."

Jackson picks up a bucket from beside him and throws water over the unconscious man. He gasps and jerks awake, thrashing against the chain like a fish on a line. Out of the corner of my eye I see Nero drop the cigarette and crush it under his shoe, driving a black mark into the concrete floor. He steps forward, the atmosphere in the room changing, as though the beating so far was just a warm-up and it's all about to kick off.

Tommy chuckles under his breath and twists his head towards me. "Hope you're not squeamish."

I say nothing. The only reason I'm even standing here is because I have to wait for Nero to give me his royal decree. I don't like to be kept waiting, and especially not when I'm waiting to go to his apartment...something I don't even want to do. So, I stand on the side lines, watching the boys' club strut around, weighing each other's balls. Although, I will say I'm curious. I want to see what

Nero does that has them all waiting on baited breath, or perhaps even they don't know.

Nero stands in front of the man. His silence might as well be a gunshot in the room. Reaching inside his jacket pocket, he removes a pack of cigarettes, taking one to replace the one he just stubbed out. His movements are slow, methodical, deliberately unhurried as he puts the packet back in his pocket and takes out the lighter. The low click gives way to the bright orange flame dancing over the end of the cigarette until it glows a bright red. I notice every tiny, inconsequential detail, because he demands it, without ever speaking a word. He has a gift, and when he finally does speak, everyone listens.

"You should know, Mr Chang, that I always get what I want." He straightens the collar of his jacket, brushing away a non-existent piece of lint.

"Not this time!" the hanging guy rasps, though it's lost on a choked cough.

Nero smiles; it's almost charming and certainly disarming. "You aren't walking out of here alive," he tells the man. Well, he's not going to tell him shit now. Don't get me wrong, he knows he's going to die, I'm sure, but hope will play tricks on the human mind. It's that fragile hope that has them spilling their guts, not a guaranteed death penalty.

"Fuck you!" The guy spits through swollen lips and broken teeth. He sways slightly as his weight shifts, and the chain lets out an ominous creak as the links grind together.

Nero sighs and then inhales on his cigarette. For the first time, I notice the way his full lips purse around it, his defined jawline flexing beneath a layer of dark stubble as he draws the breath. He turns away, giving a slight jerk of his chin to Gio, who immediately leaves the room. "One of my guys was killed in your ambush," he says, his tone completely neutral. "I think you sold me out." This time, the guy says nothing, and the only sound is the rasping of his breath. Sounds like a punctured lung to me. Nero shrugs. "Okay."

I'll admit I'm intrigued when Gio comes back in the room carrying a metal bucket. He places it at Nero's feet, where he leans down and takes out a bottle. Nero nods and steps back as Gio opens the bottle and pours it over the suspended man. It only takes a second for the smell to hit me. Gasoline. The liquid soaks the material of his jeans, cascading down his mangled body until he's coughing and choking, trying not to inhale it.

"What are you doing?" he asks, panicked.

Nero drops to a crouch, until he's almost eye level with him. "Getting what I want." He takes one final drag of the cigarette and throws it, straight at the guy's face. The ember catches and the flames tear over his body. His screams echo around the concrete room, accompanied only by the sound of the fire tearing over his skin. I'm no stranger to violence, but that's a nasty way to go. Gio moves and pulls something else from the bucket, but I can't clearly see past Nero who stands calmly, watching the burning, screaming man as if he were observing a bonfire. A hissing sound fills the room, and the flames die instantly. Gio stands to the other side of the smoking body, fire extinguisher in hand. They put him out? They set him on fire and then they put it out. Why? All I can smell is singed hair and burnt flesh, and the odour has me swallowing back bile.

Another bucket of water is thrown on him and again he jerks awake, only this time it must feel like he's imprisoned in the inner circle of hell. The scream that tears from his lips would have even the hardest of men recoiling. His skin is raw and mangled, literally as though it melted in the fire. He's completely unrecognisable, not that the round with the brass knuckles had done him many favours. Nero stares down at him.

"Painful, isn't it?" The man's unbroken moans continue. "Your lungs are incinerated from the inside, which means you're going to die. You have hours, maybe days, depending on how strong you are." He pauses, and still all the guy can do is moan.

Damn, I'd feel sorry for him if I could, but honestly, I'm simply enamored by Nero right now.

"Give me a name and I'll give you a bullet. If not, I hope you enjoy your last few hours on this earth."

"Abbiati," he sobs, the word barely comprehensible.

"Thank you." Nero removes his gun and shoots the guy in the head. The body goes limp and blood gushes into the drain. It reminds me of an animal carcass hanging in a slaughterhouse.

"Gio, Jackson, I think Bruce Abbiati needs a little visit." Nero says darkly. "Be sure to send a message." He tucks his gun back into the holster at his chest and approaches me. "Apologies for the delay." Then he walks out of the room without a backwards glance.

Nero Verdi, for all of his refinement, is a monster; one with no boundaries. To watch a man burn, to hear his screams and not even flinch...well, that puts him on my level. As if he wasn't dangerous enough to me. He's every bit as unfeeling and ruthless as I am. But he's also smart and cunning, and intelligence is the most lethal weapon a man can possess.

8

NERO

The second we're in the car I can feel her unease. She sits in the passenger with her back ramrod straight and her fingers lingering over the knife holstered at her thigh.

"Why?" she asks.

"You'll have to be more specific."

"Why are you insisting that I stay with you?"

I stare through the windshield at the headlights cutting through the darkness. "I have my reasons."

"Well, sharing is caring."

My lips twitch as I look at her again and find her intense gaze on me. "I know enough about you to know that you're very capable with some extremely powerful contacts. Right now, we've entered into something that mutually benefits us. I get what I want, and you get what you want."

"Yes, and I agreed to the exchange of services, did I not?"

"Come now, Una, don't tell me that you wouldn't look for a way out of it the second you got a chance." She says nothing. "You might pay Arnaldo a visit, or try and find your sister yourself, not that you'd get far, but still."

I pull to a stop at a red light. "I fail to see your point."

Reaching out, I trail a finger down the sharp plane of her cheek, knowing full well that it makes her uncomfortable. I've never had women complain about my touch, never met a woman that didn't beg me for it. They all want a taste of a bad boy, a walk on the wild side. If only they knew exactly what they were climbing into bed with. Una's different. She's no normal woman, and she definitely doesn't see me as the fuckable bad boy. She sees me for exactly what I am and doesn't even blink. Her skin is like satin beneath my fingertip as I trace a line to the corner of her lip, before gripping her jaw. "You stay with me, then you can't run around plotting my demise in your spare time."

A slow smile pulls at her lips, even as her eyes flash with something dangerous. "You really think you can hope to hold me against my will?"

I smirk back at her. "Oh, it won't be against your will. Because the second you get away from me, I will give Nicholai the information I have on Anna." Her breath hitches ever so slightly, her pulse throbbing erratically beneath my fingers. I allow a full-blown grin to make its way across my features. "And for all of your bravado, I don't think you want that, do you, *Morte*?" I have her, hook, line and sinker. She's got nowhere to run but straight to me. I will become her saviour and her nightmare. I'll be whatever the fuck she needs me to be if she plays the role I need her for.

Her facial expression relaxes back into one of passive indifference and outright attitude. "Okay."

"Okay?"

She pulls her face away from my grasp. "I asked for the

why. You gave it. I can appreciate a shrewd manipulator, Verdi."

Oh, we're on a surname basis now. I snort as the light turns green and I pull away.

"Of course, if you want me to do my job, then I'll need my gear. Not to mention clothes. We need to make a stop."

"Fine. Where do you need to go?"

————

THE HEADLIGHTS GLIDE across the metal roller doors of several storage units. Zeus and George sit bolt upright on the back seat, ears pricked as they stare out the windshield. I cut the engine and get out. We're in a particularly run-down part of Brooklyn. A chain-link fence surrounds the lot with two security lights on either side of the gate casting an orange glow across the concrete walkway that separates the two rows of units. Una slams the car door and starts walking, her figure casting a long shadow. There's a single security guard on the gate. This place is about as secure as a garden shed in the Bronx. What the hell is Una possibly using this place for? I scour the shadows, listening. All I can hear is the distant hum of traffic, interrupted by the occasional boat horn. I follow her, feeling the hard outline of my gun against my ribcage. My fingers itch to feel the weight of it in my hand, but I refrain. Call me paranoid but I've experienced one too many dodgy deals and subsequent shootouts in locations just like this.

The sound of one of the metal doors rolling up punches through the night air. I catch up to Una as she steps inside the open unit and flicks on a light. The back wall is lined with several metal lockers, not dissimilar to the kind you'd find in an auto shop. She takes a set of keys and unlocks one. Opening drawers, she starts removing various weapons, pulling out the clips on the pistols and checking them before sliding them back in.

"Hand me one of those bags, will you?" She points to the left-hand wall, where a couple of empty black holdalls are hanging. I had one to her and she puts god knows how many different guns in there, and then she moves on to the next drawer. Grenades. The next, knives.

"You done?"

She glances sideways at me before zipping the bag. "You know I have guns. And we're not taking down the pentagon."

She glares at me. "I like *my* guns."

"And the grenades?"

A small smile touches her lips. "Well, grenades are always handy." I shake my head as I toss the bag over my shoulder. She picks up a long steel briefcase from the corner, followed by one of the zipped duffels against the wall.

"I need that, too." She points at a black plastic case, which I pick up. "Okay, let's go." She rolls the metal door back down, snapping the padlock back in place.

"You know, you should probably find somewhere more secure to store your shit."

She walks past me. "Well, no one would store anything of value here, so no one bothers to break in." She shrugs one shoulder. She says that now.

I pull into the parking garage beneath my building and glance at Una. She hasn't spoken a word to me since we picked up her supplies, and honestly, I'm good with that. I really don't care much for her emotional wellbeing past her ability to kill. I get out of the car and open the back door, letting the dogs out. They walk to heel as I make my way to the elevator, sparing only a brief glance over my shoulder just to check she is, in fact, following.

Her footsteps behind me are so quiet it's almost unnerving. She takes 'silent as the grave' into an entirely new context.

The elevator doors open and I step in. She looks like a cornered animal when she slides in beside me, ready to bolt at any minute. She lingers slightly behind me, ever the strategist. I catch her blurred reflection in the brass doors, and even with that limited view I can see the tension in her shoulders. She's uncomfortable and fight ready.

I inspect the cuff of my jacket, adjusting the edge of my shirt. "I'm not about to jump you, Una."

"You'd be stupid to," she replies, her voice tight.

Well, isn't this going to be fun? Gio thinks I'm crazy bringing her here. He wanted me to leave her at the house, but I know there's no way she'd stay there. Well…she might, but not without slaughtering every man there who sees her face before we part ways. The tension in this small metal box becomes stifling, until I'm ready to either pry the damn doors open or point a gun at her head and tell her to stop with her shit. Luckily for both of us, the low ping rings out before the doors glide open. The dogs trot ahead, disappearing into the kitchen where Margo, my house-keeper will have left them food.

"The elevator only operates with a key, and the emer-gency exit has sensors and alarm systems on the door. So, if you run, I'll know." I look at her, making sure she sees how deadly serious I am. Honestly, I have no idea how to handle someone like her. I deal with men for whom threats and leverage will undoubtedly work. She's too calm, too accepting. It makes me suspicious. I've never had to supress someone of her skill, nor with her contacts. I'm pretty sure she could call in a favour from any big gun she likes, even Arnaldo. After all, I'm off the grid here, working on my own, and I have no doubt that she knows that. I'm just hoping that her sister is enough. True, she might be able to find Anna on her own, but I've had guys buried in the cartels for years. I'm her best bet. She steps away from me, moving to the floor-to-ceiling windows that surround the entire apartment, like a literal glass wall, imprisoning her here, high above New York.

"Your room is this way." I ascend the stairs to the second floor. The balcony style railing runs along the length of the apartment, overlooking the open-plan living space below. My step falters at the first door, the room furthest from mine, the one I had intended to put her in, but for some reason I keep walking, stopping at the one next to mine. I push the door open and hold my arm out in a sweeping gesture.

"You should have everything you need, but if not then tell me and Margo will get it."

"Margo?" Suspicion laces her voice.

"My housekeeper. I don't keep girlfriends."

She smirks. "You say that as though they're pets. Butterflies in a jar." She walks a few steps away and spins on her heel to face me. "You strike me as the sort to pluck the wings off pretty butterflies, Nero."

Una Ivanov. There's something about her that constantly taunts, teases and dares. I move further into the room, slowly closing the gap between us until I'm close enough to see her indigo eyes in the darkness. The easiest way to intimidate someone is to get in their personal space. It's a habit when trying to force someone to back down, but with Una, I find it has the opposite effect. She rises to the threat, making everything in me sit up and take note. I want to be indifferent to her, I need to be, and yet, every-thing she does captures my attention. How can it not? I've never met a woman like her, and I know I never will. There *is* no one like her. She's the best, the kiss of death herself. My eyes trace the outline of her full lips, and I suddenly remember *exactly* how they feel against mine, the lash of her tongue, the violent scrape of her teeth…

"Don't worry, I'll leave your wings well alone."

She smirks and tilts her head back to look at me. "You mistake me for something pretty and fragile, but I assure you, any wings I had were plucked a very long time ago," she says it casually, but I catch the briefest flash of sadness in her eyes. She doesn't say it for pity though; she says it because she hates to be seen as anything delicate. I shouldn't give a shit, but she's like a puzzle that I can't resist wasting my time on.

"Fine then, be an ugly caterpillar." She snorts and the briefest smile flashes over her lips, sinking a dimple into her porcelain cheek. A butterfly indeed, although her wings are made of steel and her touch may very well kill. Forcing myself to move away from her, I step out of the door.

"Nero." I halt when I hear her voice. "Uh…" she stammers over her words and it has me turning to face her. "You might hear things tonight. Don't come in here." Before I can respond, she slams the door shut.

9

UNA

"You will learn your place, Una. You are nothing and no one, an unwanted orphan. Say it!" The matron of the orphanage shouts in my face, spit flying from those thin, cruel lips. A cigarette hangs between her fingers and the smell of tobacco wafts around the room. Defiantly, I hold her stare, refusing to break. The rough wood of the chair bites against my bare thighs, exposed by the sundress I'm wearing. The leather belts that secure my wrists to the arms of the chair are worn, but they still chafe against my skin, leaving my wrists raw. The matron likes to do this, to make sure the children here are well behaved and easy. I'm not. I know what they do with us, what they have planned. I refuse to accept this fate, and above all, I refuse to accept it for my sister.

"Fine. Remember you deserve this," she growls, before taking the cigarette and stamping it into my shoulder.

It hurts, it really hurts. And then that smell, burnt flesh and melting skin. It's the first time I've smelt it, but it won't be the last.

The scene then shifts, the matron's face blurs and morphs until I'm staring at Erik. Leather restraints give way to rough hands, and the wooden chair becomes a concrete floor. I know what happens here, and already my breathing is picking up, my heart thrumming so fast I

*can barely stop myself from having a full-blown panic attack. I
thrash against the restraining hands but all it earns me is a swift slap
across my cheek. My head reels back and a sting erupts across my
skin.*

*Erik's body lands on top of me, his hot breath blowing over my
cheek. "I'm going to break you," he hisses.*

*It's at this exact moment that the part of me that still had a scrap
of faith in humanity shatters. Everything becomes a blur of torn
clothing and adrenaline. I fight, lashing out at anything within reach.
Somewhere in the chaos I become removed, and instead of experiencing
it myself, I become a bystander, and the girl being held down becomes
Anna. Only she doesn't fight, and Nicholai never arrives to save her.
Tears track down my face, and I scream as I try to get to her, but I
can't. It's as though my feet are set in concrete and all I can do is
watch as my little sister shuts down and becomes nothing more than a
fractured vessel in front of my eyes, her innocence stolen by monsters
who have no right to take it.*

Gasping awake, I drag in lungfuls of air. Tears track
down my temples, while the tell-tale ache of a scream
lodges in my throat. It takes me a second to remember
where I am. I can't remember the last time I stayed in the
same place for more than a week or two, and the constant
travelling never ceases to disorientate me. Nightmares have
plagued me for years. Well, they're not nightmares so much
as memories. My entire childhood was one long nightmare,
so I have plenty of material. This is new though. This is the
first time Anna has become the focus of my torment. That
wasn't a memory. I didn't break, but Anna would break.
The thought is enough to make my blood run cold, and a
tiny voice in the back of my mind begs me to hope, to
hope that maybe that was not her fate. I should know
better. There is no room in this world for hope, only cold
reality.

The bright lights of the city below cast a faint glow

throughout the room that throw shadows across the pale grey carpet. My pulse is still pounding, and my skin feels sticky with sweat, so I get up and silently move to the bathroom on the far side of the room. Without turning the lights on, I start the shower and strip before stepping under the hot water. Letting the darkness and water wrap around me, soothing the tension in my body. I should hate the dark, but I love it. It allows us to just be, to hide all the flawed, unsightly parts of ourselves. With the light comes the truth, the reality of our shitty existence. When I'm done, I step out onto the mat and wrap one of the thick towels around me.

After a nightmare I'm always left wide awake and unable to sleep, so I leave the bathroom and venture out into the apartment in the hopes of finding a laptop or data device of some description. To my surprise, I find all my stuff resting against one of the couches in the living room. George hops up from his bed in the corner, while Zeus studiously ignores me. Slinging the black duffel bag over my shoulder, I head back to my room, but pause when I hear a low whine behind me. George stands, watching me go with the most heartbroken expression on his face. How a supposed guard dog can be as cute as any lap dog I don't know, but he is.

"Come on," I whisper. He keeps his head low as he walks over to me and then follows me up the stairs, looking sheepish the entire time. "You're such a baby." I laugh.

Returning to bed, George curls up at the end while I dig around in the duffel bag and find a laptop at the bottom. I have a couple of locations in the city just like the storage locker in Brooklyn, as well as others around the world. Guns, passports, money, a laptop and a change of clothes to hand are always needed. You never know when a job might go wrong, and of course there's the rogue scenario. Pissing off the wrong people might result in someone putting a price on my head. The second that happens I have to disappear and run for Russia, and it's not like I can just pop home and pack a bag before I do it. This life is one where you're constantly looking over your shoulder, but it's the only one I know.

Sometimes, I'm sent after targets who seem to straddle both worlds. Cartel bosses who have a wife and kids that they kiss goodbye every morning before they step outside and kill people, peddle drugs and sell whores. I know better than anyone how that always ends, with widows and orphans. But when I see them playing at having a normal life, it confounds me. I don't understand the motivation to *be* normal, to have the standard...the human compulsion to love and be loved is such a crippling weakness, and yet, even the worst of humanity still want such a simple thing above all else. No, I can't do normal. I like the rush, the thrill of not knowing whether today might be my last. It makes each kill that much better. Every time I go after a hit, it's kill or be killed, and every time I succeed, each time I win, it makes my grey world a little brighter. My entire life is a game of survival that I am determined to conquer.

Removing the brand-new laptop from the bag, I open it. In the side pocket of the duffel is a memory stick. There's nothing on it, of course, all the information I have on the many crime organisations I work with is on my person at all times. I grab my necklace, a simple silver leaf, about half an inch long. It looks inconspicuous enough, but it's actually a locket. Inside is a tiny memory card, the kind that goes in a cell phone. I pop it into a slot on the memory stick and insert it into the USB drive. Years of information starts downloading onto the computer drive.

Four names. Four hits. I work, pouring over information until the sun starts to bleed across the grey morning sky. I learn my targets, their connections.

Finnegan O'Hara is Irish and honestly, has a knack for pissing off a lot of people. He's IRA, high up in the Irish mob in Europe and owns most of the Irish ports. If the Italians want to run drugs through Ireland, which is the easiest export point on the continent, then they have to go through Finnegan. Someone was bound to gun for him eventually. Nero seems less restrained than a lot of the mafia that I usually deal with. It doesn't surprise me that he's taking him out.

The other three: Marco Fiore, Bernardo Caro and Franco Lama are all Italian, and I have no idea why he wants them.

I'm not aware of any feuds between Nero and any of them, but then I didn't even know who Nero was until I met him. Even now, I'm not sure how he fits into all this. Lorenzo and Nero were both the sons of Matteo and Viola Santos. Lorenzo took the name and yet Nero has his mother's maiden name, Verdi, a powerful family in their own right, but with no real weight here in America. Nero had his brother killed, which is about as dysfunctional as it gets. So is it simply a family feud? If so, it's escalated pretty far, and Arnaldo is aiding it, so what's his play?

Fuck, this is enough to give me a headache. Why do I even care? I never ask for a reason behind a job. Really, these are hits like any other, except that the payment is my long-lost sister, and my employer insists on me living with him. And of course, there's the fact that I'm quite literally laying my head on a chopping block, but again, do the reasons matter? The only reason I'm doing this is to get to Anna. It matters though, because it's right there, like an alarm going off in my mind. I rely on my instincts, and my instincts are telling me that Nero is not simply the stung son of a capo, out for revenge. There's more to this. What am I not seeing?

———

I'VE BEEN HERE five days, and I've barely seen Nero. He remains in his office most of the time, while I spend all my time researching names, locations, contacts. A job like this takes a long time to put into play, and I'm still not sure how I'm going to pull it off. George sits at my feet, waiting for the crusts off my toast while I sit at the breakfast bar. I absentmindedly hand him one while skimming over the floor plans for one of Bernardo's nightclubs. The sun is just starting to rise, painting the kitchen in hues of pink and orange. I assume Nero isn't awake until I hear a faint rhythmical beat coming from somewhere in the apartment. Frowning, I get up and follow the sound, opening a door that is right next to the elevator. It's a gym, with a tread-mill, heavy bag, various weights and machinery. It must be one of the biggest rooms in his apartment, and this place isn't exactly small.

Leaning against the doorframe, I watch as his feet pound the treadmill. I can see his side profile from where I'm standing, but he doesn't seem to notice me. He's topless, his shorts riding low enough on his hips that I can make out the line of muscle that sweeps down his side before meeting the V at the front. Each muscle flexes beneath his tanned skin as he runs. Sweat glistens over every inch of him, dotting along the back of his neck before falling between his shoulder blades. I grew up training with soldiers, mostly men. I see the male form as an asset. Muscles equate to strength, nothing more. But as I watch Nero, I note the graceful way he moves, the way each line and plane of his body blends into the next. He's beautiful. There really is no other word. His body is crafted into a weapon, a destructive force of nature. And just as the perfect blade takes time to make, to balance exactly, that body is the product of dedication and sweat. He slams his hand over the stop button and the treadmill slows rapidly beneath him until he comes to a halt.

"You're staring," he says without looking at me. He swipes a towel over his face and turns to face me, his chest heaving. "That's never good where you're concerned."

"I'm not planning on killing you. Yet." I step inside the room and lean against the wall.

He smirks as he steps off the treadmill and approaches. For the first time I see the tattoos on his body, script across his chest reads an Italian proverb, which equates to something along the lines of karma is a bitch. His right arm is covered to the elbow in an intricate sleeve, but I can't make out the details without staring. He gets entirely too close as he reaches for his water bottle on the shelf right next to me. I flatten myself against the wall, but still his scent wraps around me. Sweat mixes with his body wash and he's so close to me I could literally move my hand an inch and touch him. Damp hair falls over his forehead messily as he stares down at me.

"Maybe you just like looking." Lifting the water bottle, he places it to his lips and drinks, staring at me with amusement in his eyes. A drop of sweat rolls down his throat, and I can't help but track its path down his chest. Something foreign settles in my gut and my jaw clenches. He makes me uncomfortable and yet, I want to touch him. I want to know if he feels as hard and implacable as he looks. He knows it though, because he brushes a hand over my waist. When I tense, he smiles. He thinks he's simply making me uncomfortable, but it's so much more than that.

I grip his wrist. "Don't." I warn.

He leans in until his lips are at my ear. "Or what?" he dares on a dark whisper.

Placing my hand on his stomach, I dig my nails into his skin hard enough to push him back a couple of inches. His gaze meets mine, my breath hitching as his abs tense and roll beneath my fingertips.

No one could ever argue that Nicholai isn't a master in training his assassins. He used to tell me that some guy had trained a dog, taught it to salivate on command through simple conditioning. He would ring a bell every time he fed the dog, so the dog associated the bell with food. I was trained much the same way, conditioned into having set responses. We were deprived of human touch, of even the slightest form of affection. The only time we touched another person was during a fight, under raining fists rather than soft caresses. On the rare occasion we did receive some form of contact outside of the ring it was deliberately coupled with pain, usually an electric shock. Add into the equation a lethal set of fighting skills, and the nature of human survival, and you create a reflex killer. I will admit that reflex has saved my ass more than once; however, as I got older, things changed. Much of my job involves seduction, which I was also trained in. The result is a constant battle, the instinctual versus the necessary. My instinct is to tear Nero's arm from his body, but...I don't want to.

"I'm serious, Nero."

"And yet, you're touching me." His eyes dropping to my hand splayed across his stomach. He makes no move to step away, simply waits. I realize that I can't remember the last time I touched another human being voluntarily, not to aid a job, and not to kill them. I don't know what it is about him. He's not a soldier, not a brother in arms, or a boy I grew up with. He's not really a client, and he's certainly not a hit. He is… an anomaly, an exception, a strange ally. He confuses me whilst leaving me in awe of his savagery. He leans in closer and my nails dig into his skin. His powerful heartbeat pounds through his body, ricocheting up my arm. I blink and tear my hand away from him. Huffing a small laugh, he steps back very deliberately before leaving the gym.

I stand there, confused and extremely uneasy. Weakness. This is what weakness feels like. I think he likes it. He doesn't fear me, so he wants to challenge me, wants to see me snap. Well, this living situation is going to get awkward real fast. When I go back into the living area he's not there. When he appears again he's fully dressed in an immaculate dark grey suit, his hair damp from the shower.

"I have some business to handle, I'll be back later," he says briefly, whistling at the dogs who both leap up to follow him as he walks to the elevator.

"What? You'll be back later. Are you serious?"

He turns to face me, a bored expression on his face. "You're reminding me why I don't let women stay with me."

On a laugh, I grab one of his kitchen knives and launch it at him. It nicks his jacket before hitting the steel elevator door and clattering to the floor. He cocks a brow and lifts his arm, showcasing the neat slice through the expensive material.

"Your aim is shit," he growls, stalking towards me.

"It is. I was aiming for your chest." I shrug. "Your kitchen knives aren't very well balanced. But, now I have your attention, I think we need to rediscuss our terms." He ignores me and walks straight past, heading up the stairs. I follow. "You see, you're so quick with your threats – if I leave you'll go to Nicholai. All that shit." He walks into his bedroom, ducking into the walk-in closet. Again, I follow.

"But if you go to Nicholai, he'll find Anna himself, and you'll have no leverage," I drawl, as if the entire notion is boring to me. At least then I could kill him. I stand in the doorway of the closet, watching him strip out of the damaged jacket and take an identical one off a hangar. "So…"

"So nothing," he snaps, the bite in his voice making me straighten and take note. He storms the space between us and grabs my jaw, forcing my head to the side until his lips are against my ear.

A fissure of fear settles in my chest, and I smile, feeling my heart hammer in my chest. I *feel*. Hot, angry breaths blow over my neck, and I shiver.

"Don't play games with me, Una. Don't try to negotiate or back me into a corner." His voice is deathly calm. "We both know that you want your sister a damn site more than I actually need you. But feel free to test me on it and see what happens." He releases me, shoving my face away from him and storming out of the room.

I stay there, feeling the rush of adrenaline in my system, revelling in the thrill of him. He scares me, and I like it.

10

UNA

Tommy rocks up a few minutes after Nero leaves. Strolling into the kitchen with his hands in his pockets, whistling to himself. His chestnut hair is messy and although he's wearing a suit – of course – the jacket is unbuttoned and his shirt is open to the middle of his chest. I can also smell the whisky on him from here. Sitting at the breakfast bar with my laptop in front of me, I try to form a plan to take out Marco Fiore. Nero left me a file this morning at least. Like homework. Great.

"Apparently, you and I have a hot date." Tommy winks, hopping up on a stool across from me.

"So you're babysitting me," I say without sparing him a glance.

He laughs, cocking his head to the side as he does. "Well, babysitting implies that you need supervision. I'd go more with watch duty."

I sigh. "Fine. Then you can be of use. I need you to tell me everything you know about Silk."

His eyebrows pinch together. "Marco's place?"

"Yes."

"It's a strip joint. He's there every Friday and Saturday."

Today's Wednesday. "Perfect."

"No, no, no." He shakes his head again and braces his elbows on the breakfast island as he leans forward. "You won't get him there."

Huh. So, Tommy is well aware of exactly why I'm here.

I smirk. "You do know who I am?" He stares blankly back at me. "I can get to anyone, anywhere." He shrugs and leans back in his chair. Returning my focus to my laptop screen, I study the street view outside Silk. "What about his strippers?"

"They're tight. Mostly Italian girls. It's not impossible but you might fail."

"Which fucks me for another route." I interrupt. I see him nod in my peripheral. "Security?"

He takes a cigarette packet from the inside pocket of his suit jacket. "Marco's a shady fucker. Keeps armed guys with him at all times." He takes a cigarette out and presses it between his lips as a raspy laugh works its way up his throat. "Mind you, I'd be shady if I'd made an enemy of Nero," he mumbles as he holds the lighter up, cupping the flame.

"So he did do something to piss Nero off." I can't help but probe, even though every professional facet of me is screaming not to.

Tommy exhales a long stream of smoke, a small smile touching his lips. When his eyes meet mine, I know that he knows I'm pushing. He knows that I have no idea why I'm hunting Marco. And yet...

"He supported Lorenzo." He shrugs. "He's not a fan of Nero and well, I love Nero like a brother but he has a nasty temper on him."

"So I see." *Don't ask.* "How do you know Nero?" *Brilliant.*

He leans back in his chair, eyeing me warily. "We grew up together."

"You're not Italian." For a second I think I've struck a nerve but then he simply shrugs.

"Half Italian, half Irish."

"That's unfortunate lineage." I keep my eyes on the screen in front of me. The Italians and the Irish hate each other.

He laughs. "Yeah, I was the half-breed and Nero was the bastard."

"A bastard?" *Jesus, I just can't stop.*

He takes a long inhale on the cigarette. "So they say. Anyway, we were the outcasts, so we banded together, I guess."

"Well, Italians are all about their bloodlines," I mumble.

"Aye, they are." I get up and make two cups of coffee, placing one in front of Tommy. He takes a hip flask out of his pocket and pours a little in, winking at me as he does.

"I see why you're on babysitting duty now," I remark dryly.

He shrugs. I swear he's impossible to rile. Perhaps that's more the reason why he's here instead of say, Jackson. I'm pretty sure I could goad Jackson, put him down and walk out of here without a backward glance. I swear I can already feel the walls pressing in on me. It's not the physical fact of being here; it's knowing I can't leave. The sooner I get a plan together, the sooner I can get out of here and do what I do best. Tick tock.

Tommy gets a text late in the afternoon and immediately stands up, picking up his jacket off the back of the chair. I'm grateful that he's leaving. An email from Sasha

popped up in my inbox half an hour ago and I'm itching
to read it, hoping desperately that he has something on
Anna. It's been five days. Drumming my finger on the edge
of the keyboard, I nervously wait for Tommy to leave. He
shrugs his jacket on and offers me a small salute before he
turns and walks towards the elevator. The second the doors
slide shut I pull up my email. Sasha's message has no
subject, no text, simply a link to a website.

I click on it and a website pops up. It's a webcam site
that has me swallowing back bile. It's all in Spanish and
there are various windows, each depicting a video stream. I
click on one and it shows a girl sitting on a bed. She's
completely naked with her knees pulled up to her chest.
Dark hair hangs over her face and she looks so broken, as
if every shred of hope has been stolen from her. Normally,
I wouldn't care. I'd put it down to yet another example of
the shitty world we live in and move on, but the revelation
of Anna's fate has flawed me. The girl hunches in on
herself. A bullet would be kinder than this. Steeling myself,
I keep clicking through the various windows, each one a
different dingy, concrete room, a different stained bed, a
different destroyed woman. Some of them are alone,
others have men in the room with them, and some are
being raped, their lifeless bodies being abused again and
again. I stop when I see a girl with white-blonde hair. A
man is standing in front of her, undoing his belt. She sits
on the edge of the bed, her face down and her hands in
her lap. He grabs her chin and forces her head back. The
hair falls away from her face, and I see her.

"Anna," I breathe. All too quickly it hits me, my sister
is in that place, my sister is one of those girls. I should
turn the feed off, but I can't. The man backhands her
across the face, and then he's on top of her, his jeans
shoved down past his thighs as he forces himself on her

and rapes her. Everything in me tears apart at the sight of it, and I want to look away, but I can't, because if she can endure it, then the least I can do is watch it. I wish she knew that I'm here, that I'm looking for her. The worst part is her acceptance. She doesn't fight, doesn't move, she's just given up. But wouldn't I? God knows how long she's been enduring this, over and over, day in day out. The longer I watch, the more broken I feel, until I'm right there with her, hopeless, desolate, destroyed. The pain washes over me like a tidal wave, a darkness so deep it's bottomless. Anna is in hell, and I feel like I'm right there with her, those images branded into my mind. I push to my feet and pace to the window. I want to find that man and rip his goddamn heart out of his chest. The desolation gives way to anger, and that's good. It's good. Anger is a much more manageable emotion to deal with. Startling, I reach for my knife when I sense someone right behind me. Nero's hand slams around my wrist and his eyes lock with mine as the point of the blade hovers inches from his chest.

"Honey, I'm home," he says dryly, his expression dark.

Yanking away from his grasp, I begin pacing again, trying to formulate a plan, contacts. I need to get into Mexico.

"I need to leave," I blurt. He sighs and walks over to the coffee table, glancing down at the laptop screen.

"It changes nothing."

"Are you fucking kidding me? My sister is in a dirty web brothel, being raped and beaten. I have to get her out."

He cracks his neck from side to side. "She's been there six months. She's been a sex slave for seven years. A couple more weeks won't kill her," he says, his expression nothing but icy indifference.

"You knew about this?" I whisper, pointing at the laptop. Why do I feel betrayed by that notion?

He quirks a brow. "Isn't that what we made a deal for? You kill my marks and I get your sister? As I recall, you haven't killed anyone yet." His lips set into a hard line, those dark eyes focused on me, radiating power and arrogance.

"That was before I knew where she was. I'm going for her myself." I shove past him, heading for the stairs.

"If you thought you could get her yourself, you never would have made a deal with me," he drawls. Pausing, I turn around. He hasn't moved and his back is still to me, his face twisted slightly to glance over his shoulder. "The same deal still stands, you leave and I go to Nicholai."

I rush him and he turns at the last minute, taking the punch that I land on his jaw. His head snaps to the side, and when he brings his gaze back to mine, hard, angry eyes have me taking a small step back. "You're disgusting." I spit.

"Ask yourself this, Morte... You found that website pretty quickly, considering you've been looking for your sister all this time." He rubs his hand over his jaw before slowly closing in on me. He stops when his chest is barely an inch from mine but makes no move to touch me. "Perhaps you didn't want to find her. After all, this *weakness* is what brought you right here to this very moment, at my beck and call. You could be forgiven for wanting to leave such things buried." He pulls away, staring at me with calculated indifference.

Is he right? Could I have tried harder to find Anna?

"I can't just sit in this apartment knowing what's happening to her." Everything suddenly feels too much. My skin feels tight and hot, and the walls feel like they're moving, creeping closer. I yank at the collar of my shirt, which feels as though it's suffocating me. "I need to get out."

He grabs my arm, and I lash out instinctively. His fingers slam around the back of my neck and he turns me, ramming me against the window with my arm twisted behind my back. His chest presses against me, and I can feel the rabid animal in me clawing to get out of her cage.

"Enough," he growls.

"I'm going to give you three seconds to let me go," I say calmly. Of course, he doesn't, and I jolt my head back, smashing him in the mouth. Dull pain explodes across the back of my skull, but I don't care. I lift my leg and kick off the glass, throwing us both a few yards across the room. I hear the sound of smashing as Nero hits the glass coffee table. I roll off him, completely unscathed after my broken fall. He remains dazed on the floor, and I take my chance. He's really leaving me with no options. If I stay, I risk Anna being in that place for weeks more, and one day more is a day too long. If I leave, he'll go to Nicholai and Nicholai will probably kill her. That leaves me with one option, kill Nero and run. Throwing myself on him, I straddle his waist and rain punches over his face. His lip is split from the head-butt and blood trickles over his chin. He's dazed, and I'll have to work with that. Nero is a lethal adversary, and I won't have many chances to get one up on him. I place my hand under his chin, gripping it firmly in my palm. Using the other hand I grasp a handful of his hair and twist. I pause for a second, summoning the strength needed to snap his neck. It's not as easy as it looks.

"I didn't want to have to kill you, Nero," I whisper. I truly didn't. Nero is not a good guy, but I'm not a good girl. His actions are heinous, but it's nothing I wouldn't do myself. I feel strangely connected to him, as if the darkness within us unites us somehow. How can you judge or persecute someone when they are, in effect, the reflection of yourself? I don't look at him and see his acts; I'm simply reminded of my own.

His eyes flash open and his hand slams around my throat, launching me to the side. The air leaves my lungs when my back hits the carpet and I scramble to get away, but his body lands on top of me, pinning me to the ground with his enormous weight. I fight him, attempting to buck him off and create enough space that I can get my legs around him. I can't. My nails rake over skin in the struggle, making him growl and wrap his fingers around my throat. He squeezes hard enough that I panic. My oxygen cuts off and my heartbeat rises.

Embrace death.

I hear the voice in my head, the voice of my training instructor. I can't though. My mind is too free, all the ingrained instincts I know so well are absent, and the need to survive is pounding away at me. Nero looms over me like every demon I've ever had, mocking and taunting me with my own weakness. His dark eyes watch as I flounder and fade. Black spots dot my vision. He's going to kill me.

11

NERO

Her eyes roll back in her head and I force myself to let go of her delicate neck, despite wanting to snap her like a fucking twig. She sucks in a gasping breath and her eyes open, slowly focusing on my face. "You were going to fucking kill me," I growl at her.

She frowns. "And strangling me was what? Foreplay? Get off me." She tries for authoritative but it's pathetic, really.

Wrapping my fingers around her wrists, I pull them up above her head and pin them in one hand. I brace the other hand beside her head in an attempt not to press every single part of me against her, and that's not for her benefit, trust me. This shouldn't be hot in any way, but violent women have an effect on me, and it doesn't get more violent than her. Watching her gasp for breath, my hand wrapped around that slim neck of hers...the only thing that could make it more perfect is if I were balls deep inside her. She tried to kill me and I have a fucking hard-on for it.

"I'm not doing your fucking job," she hisses through

clenched teeth, panting. Oh, she's got a mouth on her when she's pissed off.

Clenching my jaw, I bring my face close to hers, even though she refuses to look at me. Her head flails from side to side. "I took you for intelligent, Morte. You're acting like a kid trying to play hero to her sister."

She yanks against my grip, bucking her body in an attempt to break free. "You have no intention of getting her back, do you?" She fights again, but it's feeble really. She's long lost the advantage.

Grabbing her jaw, I force her to look at me. "I gave you my word, didn't I? Are you questioning me?"

"You're a liar," she says quietly. Her lips part, her tongue flashing across them for the briefest moment. I struggle to tear my eyes away from her mouth. My dick is rock-hard, and I know she can feel it. I don't care.

"I don't lie," I say absentmindedly. Her chest rises and falls heavily, pressing against me. When I meet her eyes again, they're on my mouth. Damn, she makes this difficult. Her teeth gently scrape over her full bottom lip and I fight with myself, because fuck knows this is the last woman on earth I should want to kiss, and yet, she's the only one I've ever wanted to put my mouth on this much. Women are nothing more than a moment of pleasure to me, but Una…well, Una would be a world of pleasure and pain. I want to fight her and tame her only for her to break free and do it all over again. I want to strangle her while I fuck her and then fall asleep, never quite knowing whether I'll open my eyes again, or whether she'll put a bullet between them instead. She's a challenge, the unattainable killer. I could list every reason why this is bad, but right now not a single one comes to mind. She reels me in like a magnet, and I fight it, but eventually…

Gripping her jaw, she gasps as I force her head back.

There's a beat, a moment where our eyes lock, and it's the rage there that pushes me over the edge. Mercilessly, I slam my lips over hers. Her fucking mouth. How many men have kissed her and actually lived to tell the tale? For a second she freezes, and then her lips part and her tongue darts over my bloodied bottom lip. She moans into my mouth, the sound going straight to my dick. She tries to pull her wrists free and I release her, trailing my free hand over the curve of her waist, the swell of her hip, the toned length of her thigh with the blade holstered to it. When I drop my lips to her neck, her fingers wind through my hair, pulling me closer. Her pulse pounds beneath my lips, and when I bite down on her soft skin, she physically trembles. The vicious little killer softens, purring beneath my touch. Her hips shift and she rubs against my hard dick, forcing a low groan past my lips. She's dangerous and addictive, simply kissing her is a rush of danger, and I'm quickly reminded why when I feel the cool brush of steel at my throat. Clever girl. Smirking, I slowly pull my face from her neck and stare down at her swollen, blood-stained lips and too bright eyes.

"Last chance," she says, her voice wavering.

I cock a brow, daring her. She presses the knife into my skin, the sharp sting of the blade breaking through flesh. Warm blood trickles down my throat. "I'm asking you to trust me, Una." I keep my eyes locked with hers, hoping she can see that I mean it. "Trust. Me," I growl. She looks so vulnerable, so beautifully feral.

"Never."

I push my throat harder against her blade, hissing a breath through my lips as my mouth brushes against hers. "If you won't trust my simple ability to hold up my end of a bargain, then believe in my basic sense of self-preservation." I breathe against her. "I'd have to be a stupid man to screw over the kiss of death, wouldn't I?" She squeezes her eyes shut.

"Not if you kill me."

I smile and stare at her lips. "Well, now that would be a waste." Her eyes lock with mine and she seems to be searching for something. Finally, she takes a deep breath before the blade slips away from my neck.

"Fine, but if you fuck me over, there will be nowhere you can hide, Nero."

"Such a savage little butterfly." I smirk and push off her. She rolls to her feet and says nothing, simply walks past me and heads for the stairs. I have to give her points for effort and creativity. My dick is so hard it hurts.

Heading straight for my room, I strip as I go into the bathroom. The second I'm standing under the hot water of the shower, I fist myself and start stroking over the length of my dick. Squeezing my eyes shut, a scene forms in my mind. It's so hot and twisted. I picture Una, standing over Lorenzo's dead body. She looks at me and then bites down on her bottom lip, dragging her teeth over it as she releases the soft flesh. Hopping up on the desk, she slowly glides her skirt up until the material is bunched at her waist. No underwear, just endless milky soft skin and a bare pussy. She spreads her legs wide and I get a glimpse of perfection. Her hand drops between her legs and she starts to work one perfectly manicured finger over her clit. The noise she makes has me groaning and throwing my hand against the tile to steady myself. She takes two fingers and buries them in her pussy, moaning and writhing, whispering my name. Pleasure courses through my veins and electricity rips over my body in a wave. A low growl leaves me as I come, watching it wash away down the drain.

This is what I'm reduced to, beating one out in the shower, because the deadly assassin I brought into my house tried to kill me. A beautiful woman with a homicidal streak has always been my weakness.

————

I wake to a blood-curdling scream that has me instinctually reaching for my gun before I realise it's just Una. I swipe a hand over my face and roll over, hearing another scream, and then another. Jesus. Is she being murdered? Getting out of bed, I leave my room, lingering outside her door for a second. She said not to go in there, but it's my damn apartment, and I need to sleep. This has been constant for days now. I push open the door and approach the bed. She's tossing and turning, and it looks as though she's fighting a battle in her sleep.

"Una." She doesn't wake, but the tight set of her body looks almost painful. I sigh and shove her arm. In the blink of an eye she's bolt upright and I'm staring down the barrel of a .40 cal. Of course. "Are you ever going to stop pointing guns and knives at me?" I sigh.

Her arm wavers an inch before she finally lowers it. She's left all the blinds open and the ever-present light from the city below illuminates the room. Dark shadows linger under her eyes and for once she has no smart remark for me. She drags a hand through her hair and leans against the headboard. "What are you doing in here?"

"I love to hear a woman scream, as much as the next guy, but if I'm not fucking her or hurting her, then it's just annoying." She glares at me.

"Again, you're the one that wanted me in your apartment, not me." God, she's never going to stop with that shit.

"Yeah well, I didn't expect the big bad killer to have

night terrors." Her jaw clenches, her eyes flashing angrily.
Apparently, that hit a nerve.

When I sit on the edge of the bed, she moves away
from me, shunting to the other side.

"What are you doing now?" she snaps.

"Sleeping." I lie down on the bed, ignoring her. That
vanilla and gun oil scent of hers wraps around me immediately.

"Here? You want to sleep here?" she asks, her voice
hiking.

"Your whining I can sleep through. When you're
whining you're not screaming bloody murder, so I'll
take it."

"You're an asshole," she grumbles under her breath.
Ignoring her, I close my eyes. "Nero, seriously…" She
shoves me. "You are not sleeping in my bed."

"Actually, *my* bed." I have a moment where I marvel at
what a normal conversation this is. I could almost be
friends with Una if I wasn't me and she wasn't her, but
even then, I'd still want to fuck her. Or maybe I wouldn't.
It's her bloodlust that makes my dick hard.

"I'm starting to worry that you have no sense of self-
preservation whatsoever."

I smile. "Is that a threat, Morte?"

"I don't threaten."

I smile wider. "Promises, promises."

She growls under her breath. "You're insane."

I'll get up in a minute, of course, but something about
her temper makes me smile. She's right, I am insane. I
have money, respect, power, women and a job that feeds
into all my dark and violent desires. I have everything I
want and need, and yet, Una makes it all feel boring. She's
dangerous and unpredictable. She's everything I crave
from life in one deadly package, and that might well make

me insane, but if there's one thing I've learned in life it's to accept things for what they are.

The gentle trail of fingertips over my chest pulls me from sleep. I blink my eyes open, gathering my bearings as I look around the room before glancing down to find Una's cheek pressed to my bare chest. Shit, I actually fell asleep here. Her arm is thrown over my body and her fingers glide over my left pec, before trailing down my abs one muscle at a time. I swallow hard when her palm presses flat against my lower stomach, her fingers just brushing the waistband of my boxers. Her deep, even breaths are the only thing that stops me from throwing her down on this mattress and taking her. Instead, I grit my teeth and lie there, my dick throbbing as I stare at the dark ceiling.

12

UNA

I feel the warm, solid chest beneath my cheek and listen to the strong, rhythmic heartbeat pounding like a steady drumbeat. Safety, familiarity, warmth... things I crave. Things I will never again have other than here, in my dreams with the boy I loved. It's been a long time since I dreamt of him. The weight shifts beneath me and my semi-dreamlike state starts to shatter. I don't want it to. Desperately, I try to cling to it, but the morning always comes eventually.

"Alex?" I croak, wrapping my arm more tightly around him.

"Guess again."

I jolt awake and the second I realise there's a body in the bed with me, I'm on the defensive. Reaching under my pillow, I grab my knife, before throwing myself on top of the hard body beside me. Nero doesn't even open his eyes but a wide grin works over his lips as I run the blade along his jawline. He slept in my bed! Anger has never been a problem for me. Emotions are simply a forced response born of attempting to appear normal to the outside world.

But ever since he brought up Anna, I've been out of control. I feel too much. I would say it's just her, but I don't think it is. He has the ability to rile me where no one else ever has. He brings things out in me that I didn't even think existed. I feel like a ball of thread and Nero is just pulling and pulling, unravelling me. And eventually, all that will be left is a tangled mess, impossible to put back together again. He scares me, and I long for my cold indifference, my dark hole where nothing and no one can possibly touch me. His eyes flash open, ensnaring me instantly.

"Careful, Morte."

"Or what?"

He grips my hips and his body rolls beneath me, pressing his hard dick right into the apex of my thighs. Warmth unfurls low in my stomach, and I frown. One of his hands wraps around the back of my neck and he wrenches me forward until we're face-to-face, the blade between us. My heart pounds in my chest and I close my eyes for a second, listening to that rhythmic pulse hammering in my ears. Life. Electricity.

"Look at me," he demands. I meet that dark gaze of his, normally so calculating. The whisky colour of his irises swirl, morphing into a honey gold. Wrapping his fingers around my wrist, he squeezes hard and forces the blade away from his throat. I swallow heavily, dragging in much needed oxygen. It's like he's vacuuming all the air from the room with just a look. My mind flashes to that kiss yesterday. I only wanted to render him weak, but the brutal brush of his tongue, the way he takes without apology... I've never felt so out of control, and I've never wanted that lack of control so much.

His thumb brushes over the side of my neck just as I feel the sharp scratch of the blade over my collar bone.

Perhaps I should feel threatened, but I don't. Everything slows and I smile as I stop thinking, and just feel. I feel the frantic rush of adrenaline and desire swirling and mixing into something so potent, it cripples me.

My entire being focuses on the exact point where his hot skin presses against the insides of my thighs, where the blade ominously lingers. His free hand glides over my thigh and I grit my teeth, fighting my quickening breaths. I tell myself to pull away, because part of me wants to walk this line with him. A gasp tears past my lips when his fingertips brush the seam of my underwear. His gaze brands me as he studies my every move, every tremble, every desperate breath. When his fingers slip beneath the thin material, my hand darts out, grabbing his arm and forcing him to pause. Cocking a brow at me, he twists my wrist, causing the blade, still clutched in my fingers, to drag over my chest in a burning line. My breath hitches and blood wells before spilling slowly over my skin. My grip on him softens enough that he brushes over my wet pussy, leaving me physically shaking as the opposing voices in my head reach a crescendo. The moonlight spilling through the windows plays over the smirk on his lips before he roughly presses two fingers inside me. My eyelids shutter on a ragged breath.

"Fucking look at me." His voice rumbles through the darkness and my eyes snap open.

He holds me hostage, watching me as he pulls his fingers out and then thrusts back in. My mouth falls open on a silent moan that hitches in my throat and everything slips away. Logic and reason cease to exist and all that matters is that he makes me feel this need; he makes me want him in this all-consuming way. Nero is danger and lust, rage and desire and I shouldn't like it, but I do. Our eyes lock as his fingers move inside me, sending me hurtling towards a precipice. The knife digs into a point in the centre of my sternum and heat tears through me as the thrusting becomes more aggressive. My core tenses just as a moan slips past my lips.

"Come for me, Morte." He groans and the intensity presses in on me until I fall apart, feeling his eyes on me and moaning incoherently as my nails claw over his skin.

I remain there, on my knees, my hands braced against his solid chest as I attempt to catch my breath. I've never felt anything like that, never felt so completely owned by someone. The knife disappears and he brings his fingers to his lips, smearing moisture over them before sliding them in his mouth. My heart stutters over itself, and I'm caught between being embarrassed and consumed with a debilitating want. I can't take my eyes off his mouth as his tongue flashes out over his lips. Then he pushes up off the mattress until our faces are a mere breath apart, his lips brushing over mine teasingly. His tongue strokes over my bottom lip until all I can taste is myself. His cock is pressing against me and it has me faltering, the trance slipping.

"I…" I start, but I have no words. Climbing off him, I rush for the bathroom, seeking some space, some clarity. I go to slam the bathroom door but he's there, blocking it.

"Don't do that shit," he says calmly, the desire I saw in his eyes only seconds ago replaced with a simmering anger.

"Get the fuck out, Nero," I snap.

"Who's Alex?" he asks.

What the fuck? The mention of his name has memories flashing through my mind in a burst of images. Brown eyes, an easy smile, safety, warmth, love, and then horror and heartbreak, death and destruction.

"Someone I killed."

Nero watches me through narrowed eyes and his jaw sets in a hard line. I don't want to talk to him about Alex, because in a strange way he reminds me of him. *It's the eyes; they have the exact same colored eyes*. That's where the similarity ends though. Alex was kind and good. Nero is bad and cruel. Alex was the light to my dark. Nero would be the pitch-black shadows that linger even in the darkness, calling to me, enticing me.

We stare at each other for a few seconds before I cock a brow at him. "I need to shower." The numbers on the bedside clock glow, showing that it's only five thirty in the morning, but I don't care. I'll take any excuse to get away from him.

"Tommy's busy today, so I'm taking you to a meeting with me," he says out of the blue.

I want to tell him to stick it, because I'm not one of his soldiers, but honestly, the thought of getting out of this apartment is far too good to pass up.

"Fine. Now, get out." He drags his eyes over my body without an ounce of shame and then turns and leaves. Sighing, I brace my hands against the vanity, staring at my reflection in the mirror. I jagged line runs from my collar bone to the centre of my chest, just above my tank top. It's just a scratch, and it's nearly stopped bleeding already.

I don't want to think about Nero and what just happened in there. It's more concerning to me that I thought he was Alex. That's disturbing on so many levels, but mostly because Alex was the only person who ever made me feel safe, an instinctual bone-deep safety, an implicit level of trust. Nero made me feel that same safety for just a few seconds, and I don't like it because it feels like he's taking something from Alex, something he has no right to take. Alex may be long gone, but he will always be that boy for me, he has always been 'the one'. Some people have a past, demons…mine ride on my shoulder constantly waiting for an opportunity to take a bite. I've done awful things, and truthfully, I tell myself that I did them to survive, because I had to, but there is no such thing as having to. There is always a choice. I chose to survive, whatever the cost, even when it cost Alex's life. What is the price of one human soul? Because I'm sure by now I don't have one. Any soul I do have left I'm willingly selling to Nero. If the devil were a person then it would undoubtedly be him.

I spend a couple of hours in my room, avoiding Nero. He's waiting in the kitchen with an espresso in his hand, wearing a suit that hugs every graceful line of his body. I wonder if anyone actually falls for his sophisticated façade. Don't get me wrong, he's intelligent and a shrewd negotiator, not to mention manipulative, but beneath all the cunning civilities he's feral and blood thirsty, the most basic of animal qualities. I've never felt that more than when his eyes were on me and his fingers in me, his name on the tip of my tongue. I want to be appalled by him, but the worse his is, the more captivated by him I seem to become. His eyes flick up briefly and he studies me while sipping on his coffee. A small frown line sets between his brows.

"If you even think about asking me to dress like that..." I point at him. "I'm going to cut you." His lips twitch and he wisely keeps his mouth shut. Pulling the clip out of my gun, I place it on the breakfast bar, loading three more bullets into it then clicking it back into place. I can feel his eyes on me.

"What?" I growl without looking up.

"This isn't really a gun kind of meeting."

Placing my gun in my holster, I lift my gaze to him. "It's that kind of attitude that will get you killed."

WHEN WE GET to the parking garage, Tommy is leaning against a black Range Rover. He grins at me. "Una, you are looking ravishing today."

"Fuck off."

Laughing, he opens the back door of the SUV, but Nero places his hand on the small of my back, leading me away. I quickly shrug off his touch, glancing over my shoulder to see the dogs jump in the SUV.

"First babysitting me, now you have him chauffeuring your dogs." I snort. "What did he do to piss you off?" The lights on a black Maserati flash and I go to the passenger door.

Nero glances at me over the top of the car, his expression its usual unreadable mask. "It keeps him out of trouble."

I get in the car as he slides behind the wheel. "Better to find trouble than be driving dogs around."

The engine purrs to life. "In this city, there is nothing more dangerous than being Irish *and* Italian," he says quietly.

"You care about him."

"In order to lead you must be loyal to those who follow you. My guys work for me, and I protect them." He reverses the car out and puts it back in gear. "That's the mafia."

There's something about him that has me perplexed. The mafia would never truly accept Tommy. Like I said, they're all about bloodlines. And from what I know of Nero, he's not exactly popular in the mafia himself. Respected? Yes. Feared? Certainly. Liked? No. I still haven't worked out what his play on this entire situation is, and with my sister in the balance, I want to know.

"Is that what all this is about, the mafia?" I ask, feigning only vague interest. "Your loyalty to them?" The muscles in his jaw tighten and then spasm beneath his skin. He says nothing, so I ramp up the pressure. "You've managed to climb pretty high...for a bastard." The second I speak the words I feel the air shift, like the crackle of electricity in the atmosphere before a storm. Outwardly, he doesn't move. His gaze remains fixed on the road, but his posture tenses, his knuckles turning white on the steering wheel.

"Stop talking, Una," he says on a low growl.

I'm close. "I want to know what a bastard enforcer is doing with the underboss of the Italian mob. I want to know how someone of your stature was able to dig up my sister. How is it that you have your own brother killed and manage to walk into being capo?" The car slams to a halt before we even exit the parking garage, thrusting me forward against my seatbelt. We sit for a second, the engine idling, and neither of us saying anything. He turns that icy glare on me, pinning me to the spot.

"If I wanted you to know anything, I would have told you. I don't trust you, Morte."

"And you're not telling me anything, so I don't trust you."

He smirks. "Just remember that this situation is mutually beneficial. I don't give a fuck if you trust me, I don't need you to, you don't need me to. Simply trust in the fact that I have something you want and you have something I need."

"Lies. You don't need me. My bullet or yours, they both end the same way. You need someone to blame. I'm not sure whether I should be offended or flattered that I'm the one whose back you've decided to put a target on."

His eyes trace over my face, my lips, my throat. I feel like a rabbit caught in a trap, waiting for the big bad wolf to take a bite. "You're everyone's exception," he says simply.

"What?"

"Arnaldo, Nicholai, the cartel...they all turn a blind eye to you."

I lift my chin defiantly. "Because I'm neutral. I told you, I don't take sides."

"You're not taking sides now."

Oh, but I am. For Anna. And for all of me saying I don't trust Nero, weirdly, I think I do. Every rational fiber of me knows he's dangerous. Every ingrained piece of training is screaming that I know better. And yet...aren't we already allies in a twisted way? I killed his brother and essentially made him capo. He found my sister where I never could, and now we're here, bartering, tentatively trying to outmaneuver each other. The thing is, I trust him more *because* he's blackmailing me. I may not understand his motivations, but I know that he wants something and is prepared to give in exchange. It's a simple concept.

"And now my sister is in hell, but you won't help her until I kill your list, all of whom are practically untouchable."

"If there is one thing I have witnessed in this world, it's the lengths people will go to for love. Even death herself is affected by its illness," he says coldly.

"Are you going to tell me what you're doing to get Anna back?"

"No, just know that I can pull strings and reach people that you couldn't hope to yourself." He leans in, stroking a finger down my cheek. I tear my face away from him but he grips my jaw, dragging my face towards him. If I wanted to, I could break his wrist, but I don't. All I should feel is hate, and loathe his touch, but I don't, because when he touches me like this, I don't feel the usual ingrained instinct to kill. It's as though all my conditioning can be overridden by his cruelty. It's a strange thing, to never be able to tolerate human touch. And the second that I can, I crave it, no matter its form. Nero is this warped exception to everything I know, as though he is above the law of physics themselves.

"And now I'm your Russian dog, chained and leashed, doing your bidding," I whisper.

He drags me to him, brushing his lips over mine. "You're not a dog, Una. You're a dragon, a thing of myth and whispers." His teeth graze my bottom lip and a ragged breath falls from my lips. "You ask me what I want. It's simple. I want power. With you, I will burn everything to the ground." A maniacal smile works over his lips and that darkness of his calls to me on every level, to the monster that I am. His fingers squeeze harder, forcing my head back. I relish in the touch because it's hard and angry, passion laced with hate.

"How?"

"Power is nothing more than a game of strategy, a chessboard. You are my queen, Morte, the most valuable piece on the board."

"Queen protects king," I whisper. Or in this case, the queen is a body shield for the king.

"Queen takes all." His fingers dig into my cheeks before his lips press against mine, rough and brief before he shoves me away from him like an unwanted toy.

13

NERO

"Stay in the car." I throw the door open. She gets out and I glare at her over the roof. "Was I speaking a foreign language?"

She cocks a brow. "I didn't leave your apartment to sit in your car."

"I didn't bring you with me for a day trip. I brought you because Tommy is busy –"

"Ah, yes, driving Zeus to his appointment with a tree to take a piss on."

"– and you can't be trusted on your own."

"So now I'm the untrustworthy one? As I recall, I came of my own free will."

"Fucking women, you're all the same, don't listen to shit," I grumble, turning my back and heading towards the stairwell.

"Careful, capo. I'm the one who brought the gun, remember?" She falls in step beside me, and low and behold, she has her gun strapped to her damn thigh.

"This is a government building."

"So, take the service entrance."

Stopping, I grab her arm, turning her to face me. She tenses and I smirk. I've learned with her, that it's the casual touches that make her uncomfortable. Grab her by her throat or grip her arm hard enough to break it and she's fine. Finger-fuck her, and it's tentative, but it seems pleasure can tamper her bloodlust. "This is not a tactical assault. I told you, it's not a gun affair. It's a meeting."

"I thought that was mafia code for kill someone." She raises both eyebrows as though this should be obvious.

"What? No." I shake my head. "Jesus. Look, lose the gun or wait in the fucking car." She rolls her eyes and unbuckles the holster from around her thigh, dropping to a crouch and sliding it across the parking garage floor until it comes to a halt beneath the car fifty yards away.

"Happy?" she scowls. I eye the cuff at her wrist. "Don't even think about it." She struts past me, hips swaying in a way that I don't think she's even aware of. Damn, her ass looks good in those pants.

I have a meeting arranged with Gerard Brown, otherwise known as the current Port Authority Chief. Of course, he doesn't realize it's me he's meeting with, simply the director of Horizon Logistics, a legitimate company that, as it happens, I own. His secretary shows us to his office, eyeing Una the entire time. I don't blame her. Nothing about Una fits into normal society unless she's forced to. Give her a job, tell her she has to play the mayor's wife and she'll pull that shit off no problem, but in her natural state, people become wary of her. It's the same way an antelope can sense the presence of a lion. Their instincts tell them she's dangerous and yet they trust what their eyes see, that she's just a tiny, pretty little woman.

Gerard Brown is a middle-aged guy with a beer gut, an ill-fitting suit and a moustache that looks like he stole it from the set of a seventies porn film. That said, this is the man that controls all of the docks in New York City. Nothing comes in or out without his say-so, and it just so happens that Finnegan O'Hara has his say-so. Whether he knows about the nature of O'Hara's dealings, it's impossible to say.

"Mr Brown. Thank you for seeing me on such short notice." He holds his hand out and I shake it. His thick eyebrows pull into a frown, and he squints behind his glasses.

"I'm sorry, you'll have to forgive me, but I don't know your name. My secretary –"

"Was never told it," I finish for him, taking a seat in the leather chair across from him. He sits and places his palms flat on the desk, subtly glancing at Una where she stands with her back to the wall, placed exactly between the window and the door. "I am Nero Verdi."

His face pales and he leans back in his chair, trying to put as much distance between us as possible. "Mr. Verdi." He tugs at his collar and a thin sheen of sweat blossoms on his skin.

I cross my ankle over my knee and brush my pant leg with a smile. "I see my reputation proceeds me. Good. This should go quickly then." He squeezes his eyes shut and swallows heavily. "You have a working relationship with Finnegan O'Hara."

"Please. I don't want any trouble –"

"You handle his shipments, which means you know when the next one's coming in...when he's coming in. No?"

He shakes his head. "No, I don't know."

"What kind of chief doesn't know what's coming into his own ports?" I fix my gaze on him and he visibly flinches. This will be easy.

"Please, I don't –"

"You're boring me." Una sighs, pushing off the wall. She grabs him around the throat, shoving him back in the chair as she takes a seat on the desk. "When is he coming into the city?" Nothing. "I'm going to count to three," she says the words so sweetly. "One, two, three." The blade at her wrist drops into her hand and she grips it, driving it towards his face. He shrieks and braces. There's a beat of silence, a tense moment before he opens his eyes and finds the point of the blade poised millimeters from his right eye. She wraps her free hand around the back of his neck and pulls him towards her, cradling his head against her chest as if he were a small child. "You don't need your eyes to talk, Gerard," she whispers before stroking her fingers down his cheek. She then puts the blade away and hops down off the desk, returning to her spot by the wall.

I glance over my shoulder at her and adjust in my seat because my dick is uncomfortably hard. Damn, it's the way she handles everything, so calm, yet so psychotic. Turning back to face Gerard, I cock a brow at him. He's trembling and about to spill his guts, because if he doesn't, Una will cut his fucking eyes out of his head. I know it and he knows it.

———

UNA BRISTLES with attitude and impatience as I step into the elevator. Accordingly, I'm agitated and pissed off. My skin feels too tight for my body and my dick will not let up. My balls are starting to ache, bringing about a whole new meaning to blue balls.

The second the doors glide shut I turn on her, pressing my hand against the centre of her chest and shoving her against the mirrored wall of the elevator. Her eyes narrow but she makes no other move to stop me. "At any point, did

I ask for your help?" I'm not really pissed off about it. I'm pissed off because I want to fuck her, but that's not rational.

She slaps my hand away from her chest, which just serves to eliminate the only thing between us. Her chest brushes against mine, the tension in this confined metal box becomes stifling. "The civilized bullshit doesn't suit you." She smirks, dragging her gaze from my eyes to my lips and back again. "Don't pretend you're not every bit as monstrous as I am, Nero." She strokes her hand down my chest, my stomach, skimming over my crotch. I clench my teeth and suck in a sharp breath. "You're worse."

Her lips barely touch mine and I have to bite back a groan. Fuck, fuck, fuck! For a second, I lose track of everything that isn't her, her tight body, her perfect lips, her lethal words. And then I manage to get a handle on it. Just.

"I am," I agree, stepping back and smoothing a hand down the front of my jacket. "But cutting people's eyes out…" I tilt my head to the side. "It's not the mafia way."

The elevator pings and the doors slide open. She strides past me. "You know the thing that pisses me off about the mafia?"

"I'm sure you'll enlighten me."

She stops next to the car, spinning on her heel to face me. "If you're bad, just be bad. Why wear a white hat?"

Before I can respond, she drops to her knees on the dirty concrete of the parking garage and I lift a brow. She rolls her eyes. "Not likely," she grumbles before lowering herself to the ground and reaching underneath the car, coming back out with her gun. She climbs to her feet and fastens it back in place. Huh, I never realized how naked she looked without it until she put it back on. My vicious butterfly. My lethal queen.

14

UNA

"So, Finnegan's going to be here in three days?" Leaning back in my seat, I pull one knee up, bracing my boot against the edge of Nero's expensive leather.

"Yeah, him and half an army of IRA guys."

The car winds through the streets of New York and the sun is just starting to drop between the skyscrapers, painting the sky in streaks of pink and purple. "Bernardo and Franco aren't in the city for another two weeks," I murmur.

"Okay, so we hit O'Hara, then Marco, and wait for Bernardo and Franco."

"Oh, it's 'we' now?"

"It's always been 'we'," he remarks quietly while turning the car at a junction. "You aren't doing this *for* me, Morte. You're helping me, so I help you. Remember that."

He's a bastard, he really is. His phone rings, the sound blasting from the car speakers loudly. He clicks a button on the steering wheel.

"Yeah?"

"Boss, I have a gentleman here who wants to talk to you. Seems the Los Carlos think they're getting an unfair deal." I think it's Jackson, and even I can hear the amusement in his voice. He's the only one of the three whose voice I'm not very familiar with.

"Where?" Nero asks.

"The club."

"On my way." The line goes dead and he turns the steering wheel hard, sending the car screeching down a side road.

"Trouble in paradise?" I drawl.

He looks at me and holds my gaze far longer than he should considering he's driving. "Par for the course, Morte."

The Los Carlos are a smaller gang here in the city, heavily involved in drugs and seemingly supplied by Nero. The Italians have always run the cocaine trade in New York and they probably always will.

Eventually, he pulls the car up outside of a dirty looking little club in Hunts Point, South Bronx. A couple of guys in suits linger just outside the door, guns in hand. When Nero gets out of the car they speak in quick fire Italian. This isn't my business and has nothing to do with why I'm here. I should stay out of it, and yet I find myself opening the door. Morbid curiosity has me climbing out of the car. I pull my hood up as I follow Nero to the door, and he makes no move to stop me.

Inside, it's just as much of a shithole. The floors are sticky and the walls and ceiling are so tarnished with nicotine they're stained a dull brown. Smoke seems to hang in the air as if it's a permanent feature. An old jukebox in the corner is playing some soul music quietly, and in front of us, sprawled across the black and white tile floor are two bodies. Both are Latino, and neither of them can be older than twenty. Jackson stands with his back to us, toe to toe with another kid. This one is maybe twenty-five at a push. He squares up to Jackson, gun in hand. Ten other guys are fanned out behind him, standing amongst the scattered tables and chairs that fill the bar. It looks like the scene of some cliché gangster film.

Nero pulls out a chair and takes a seat. Slowly reaching inside his jacket pocket, he takes out a packet of cigarettes, sliding one free. Everyone in the room has their eyes on him, watching, waiting. He places the cigarette between his lips and lights it. The heavy click of the lighter snapping shut is like a gunshot in the room. The guy across from Jackson starts to fidget and Jackson moves away, coming to stand behind Nero. The smirk on his face is part mocking and part genuine amusement. I remain completely removed off to the side of the room with my back to the wall. The safest place you can ever be is with a wall at your back, because people can't walk or shoot through walls.

Nero still says nothing and the tension in the room makes the young guy squirm. "Look, man, we want a bigger cut. Forty percent." He shifts his shoulders from side to side, acting the big man.

Nero leans forward, bracing his elbows on spread thighs. The cigarette hangs between his fingers, spilling ash onto the tiled floor. He couldn't look any more out of place here if he tried. So perfect in his expensive suit, immaculate and beautiful, dark and deadly. Ten armed men face him and yet he never looks out of control. He never ceases to be the ultimate danger in the room.

Sighing, he gets to his feet and holds his hand out. Jackson wordlessly places a gun in Nero's waiting palm. They all reach for their weapons, but he remains relaxed, arrogant as he walks up to the kid and stares him in the eye before lifting the gun to his head. The kid opens his mouth, his eyes going wide...BANG. My fingers are wrapped around my gun, ready, waiting for the impending hailstorm of bullets. It doesn't happen. Yet.

"This is my fucking city!" Nero roars, eyeing them one by one. "And if you bite the hand that feeds you, I will put you down like a rabid dog." He points his gun at the ground and fires off two more shots at the dead body of their former leader. "Does anyone else want a bigger fucking cut?"

No one says anything. He hands the gun back to Jackson and straightens the cuff of his shirt. So civilized, yet so feral. "Now, if I have to come down to this shithole again, if I so much as hear a whisper of a problem..." He looks up, his expression speaking of destruction and war. "I won't kill you. I'll kill your wives, your girlfriends, your fucking children and your mothers." His voice gets steadily louder until it's like thunder, rumbling off the walls. "I suggest you don't test me." And then he turns his back and walks out.

Some people make threats, meaningless words and posturing. But Nero's soulless, and anyone can see it. When he says he's going to slaughter your family, you damn well believe him. Whoever said it wasn't better to be feared than respected? Somehow he achieves both.

"So was that the mafia way?" I follow him to the car. He simply glares at me and gets in. I snort. "I thought you guys were all about leaving the women out of it."

"I play by a different set of rules."

Indeed, he does. Nero Verdi will use whatever he has at his disposal to keep people in line, honour or ethics be damned.

"You know, it's situations like these where you should probably have your own gun," I say, fastening my seatbelt.

He starts the car. "Haven't you figured it out yet,

Morte? I don't need guns. I only have to say the word and someone dies." And I can't help but be in awe of his sheer arrogance. To stand in the middle of ten guys and shoot their leader in the head. It's like he's invincible.

By the time we get back to the apartment, Tommy is already there, waiting. George runs up to me as soon as I walk in the door, whining excitedly. Taking a seat at the breakfast bar, I open my laptop, staring at the minimized window in the bottom left corner. Anna. Maybe it's just a twisted brand of self-torture, but I click it, opening up the box. She's lying on the bed, alone this time. Her too thin body curled in on itself. Seeing her so fractured makes my very soul hurt. I press my palm against my forehead and rest my elbow on the side, staring at the image of her.

"Una." I hadn't heard Nero come up behind me, which is all the proof I need that I'm not focused. Anna complicates things, but I can't see past her. He reaches around me and clicks a button, closing out the window. "Don't look at it," he says quietly. His body lingers so close, right behind me without touching. He brushes my hair off my shoulder, but again, his fingers never make contact with my skin. For a second, I find myself wanting his touch, but he steps back and all I hear are footsteps as he walks away. I need focus. Pain and blood, the promise of death. I need to remember what I am, to feel that cool indifference, the methodical application of force and consequence. I can't save Anna and I need to take it out on someone, or something.

I find myself in the gym, staring at the heavy bag. Plugging in my iPod, I blast heavy rock until the beat rumbles the floor beneath my feet. Cracking my neck from side to side, I go to town. The force of my bare fists colliding with the canvas of the bag quickly has my knuckles splitting. Blood coats the bag and my fists, but I don't care. I like the pain, the feeling of age-old scar tissue tearing apart again and again. I stop only when my body is soaked in sweat and my lungs are heaving for breath. A brush of contact on my arm has me whirling around, fists raised. Nero smirks, but the expression slips and his eyes narrow as he looks at my blood-stained hands.

"Tearing your fists up isn't going to get her back any faster," he remarks dryly. That uncomfortable feeling settles in my chest again, so I turn and hit the bag. Getting in three strikes before his arms wrap around me and he crosses my own arms over my torso, pinning them in place. I fight to get free, but just end up fighting myself. His breath blows over my neck in slow even draws. "Stop, Morte."

"Fuck you, Nero." My voice cracks slightly, frustration and helplessness seeping through.

He huffs a laugh and releases me. I whirl to face him and his eyes lock with mine for a beat before he slides his jacket off his shoulders and starts yanking at his tie. Dropping them to the floor, he then begins to unbutton his shirt. The material parts, revealing tanned skin over hard muscles. Tattoos appear beneath the veneer of his expensive suit.

"You want to hit something?" He spreads his arms wide. "Don't pretend you don't want a shot at me."

He moves, and I trace over the tight muscles of his stomach, bunched and ready. Clenching and releasing my bloodied fists, I mimic his movements. The corner of his lip twitches and an infuriatingly cocky smirk appears. I was always taught that if outmatched or outsized by an opponent, let them come to you. Defend, then attack. Right now though, I don't listen to any of it. The urge to take out every inch of my frustrations on Nero's perfect face drives me. I lunge and land a punch to his jaw. His head snaps to the side and he spits out a mouthful of blood.

"Feel good?" he asks on a grin.

"Not nearly enough." I hit him three more times and he let's me, before rearing back and nailing me in the gut. I cough and stagger back a step as I force my lungs to drag in a breath despite my paralyzed diaphragm.

He cracks his neck to the side and bounces on the balls of his feet, his arms hanging loose at his sides. "Don't think I'll go easy on you because you're a girl." We go toe-to-toe, catching each other with blows and ducking away. He grabs me around the throat and uses it to pull me close to him.

"So vicious, Morte," he purrs, his breathing heavy. I gasp for air and his eyes drop to my lips. He inches closer, until I punch him in the gut. Grunting, he lets go and hits me hard in the face. The taste of blood in my mouth elicits a laugh. I lunge towards him again but he swipes my legs out from under me, my back hitting the unforgiving floor of the gym. I roll onto my front, ready to push up, but he lands on my back, his entire weight pushing me into the mat beneath me.

One hand wraps around my throat from behind, whilst the other grips my hip. He's shameless in pressing his dick against my ass, rolling his hips against me. Lust and rage are so very close together, mixing and swirling into some-thing explosive and raw. His lips brush over the side of my neck and hot, erratic breaths blow over my skin, making me shiver. "You done?" he asks in a patronizing as fuck tone.

Fuck him. I try to jab my elbow into him but can't do shit from where I am. He laughs and grabs both my arms, pinning them down beside my hips. His body shifts, and he slides away from me. Warm lips touch the exposed strip of skin at my lower back and I gasp, shaking beneath the brief contact. He flips me over and my skin erupts in goose bumps when his lips skate over my hipbone now. The bloodlust wavers for a second, giving way to an entirely different kind of lust. I grab a handful of his hair and use it to pull his face up. His eyes follow the length of my body, and the look in them has my resolve wavering. His palms inch over my stomach, pushing the material of my top up as he goes. My heart pounds, the rhythm getting faster and faster the higher his hands move. By the time his face is hovering over mine, I can barely breathe. Blood trickles from the corner of his lip and already his jawline is splotched in angry red marks.

When his lips crash over mine, he starts an entirely new fight. Teeth rake over my split lip and I hiss at the sting, gripping his hair and pulling hard. Winding his fingers around my jaw, he cranks my head back, forcing my lips to part wider for him. He doesn't just kiss me, he throws down a gauntlet, declaring war with every violent swipe of his tongue. I shove against his chest and he pulls back an inch. That's when I slap him, yes, I slap him like a girl. His head twists to the side before he very slowly brings his gaze back to mine. Those whiskey irises swirl dangerously and there it is; fear, reaching out with cold fingers. I smile and lean into its touch, relishing in the frantic pounding of my heart, the instinctual trembling of my body. Nero scares me and it's such a rare gift, one that no one else has ever given me.

Grabbing me by my throat, he wrenches me off the floor, tearing my shirt over my head before dropping me like dead weight. Then he's yanking at the button of my pants, dragging them down my legs. I barely get a chance to think about what that means before he's over me again, his hard body between my legs and his rough lips moving against mine.

He has me in a trance of sorts, caught somewhere between lust and rage. All I can feel is him, all I can think about is his hands on me, his tongue in my mouth, his raw brutality. I want to be on the receiving end of Nero. I need him at his worst, to make me fear him, and he gives me all of that and more, demanding and taking what he wants from me. Under his touch I feel alive. *I feel.* All my training, my past, my wariness of him, everything I know I should do…it all disappears. All that matters is this exact moment. It's the kind of weakness that gets you killed, but I can't even summon the will to care.

I hear the clink of his belt buckle, feel the harsh grip of his fingers on my hips, the tearing of material. And then nothing but the hot press of his cock against me, pushing, threatening. Wrenching my hips up, with almost no warning, he slams inside me in one brutal thrust. All the air leaves my lungs, and my nails rake over the back of his neck, making him growl like the feral beast he is. My pussy clenches around him as shock waves ripple through my core. I've never felt so utterly invaded and it's both uncomfortable and welcome. His forehead falls to mine and I close my eyes, inhaling a staggered breath, breathing in the scent of his cologne, the hint of cigarette smoke.

A broken groan works its way up his throat. "You feel so fucking good, Morte." He pulls out and pushes back in, dragging a gasp from me. "So fucking tight," he growls against my mouth.

I want him to stop talking and just fuck me, so I press my lips to his. He groans into my mouth, slamming his hips into me, pushing me to the point of pain on every thrust. I like it, I need it. The pain is what drives me; the pain is what pushes me to the limit. The more he fucks me, the more rabid he gets until his fingers are digging into my skin and his kisses become bites. Everything about him savage and animalistic. He fucks me like he's trying to kill me, and I embrace the threat, daring him on as he wages sweet war on my body. I bite his bottom lip and my mouth fills with the metallic tang of his blood. My core starts to tighten, winding up and up until I feel like I can't take any more. One hand dives into my hair, wrenching my head back. His other hand slips between our bodies, where he pinches my clit at the same time he bites down on my neck, hard. I lose it. Screaming, writhing, shattering apart beneath him.

"I want to tear you apart," he growls, pinching my jaw between his teeth. The orgasm reigns on and on, slowly tearing me apart before putting me back together again. My body falls limp, and he drives into me hard and fast three more times. Then his head falls back, and the sound that leaves his lips is so guttural, so primal, that it makes me shiver. The roped muscles of his neck pop out and then his abs tense as his body jerks. I've never seen a man look more vulnerable or more powerful than he does in this moment. He finally stills and pitches forward, bracing his hands on either side of my body as his chin touches his chest. A drop of sweat rolls down the center of his chest, winding between the angry claw marks that mar his skin.

It's only when my pulse slows and the aftermath of my orgasm fades that I start to feel uncomfortable. I just fucked him. And that's the last thing I need to be doing with Nero Verdi of all people. He just…he makes me burn for him. He feeds into every element of my nature, stoking the flames of my violence until it's an inferno. We're fire and gasoline, the perfect combination, the perfect disaster.

"*Now* do you feel good?" He cocks a brow.

Feigning indifference, I roll my eyes and shove him off

me, climbing to my feet. I don't even bother putting clothes on. I just walk straight through the apartment and head to my room.

When I've showered, I lay in bed, staring at the ceiling. I don't even know what I'm doing anymore. It feels like everything I once was is slipping away, and I'm becoming something else entirely. I'm Una Ivanov, the kiss of death, ruthless, efficient, professional. It's like that person doesn't even exist here, in this apartment. I'm becoming someone who acts on impulse, without thought, driven by emotion and...cravings. That hardened mask I've worn for so many years now evades me, and I'm not sure I want it back. It's true that not feeling anything always kept me safe, focused, efficient, but it's like Nero pressed a defibrillator to my chest and shocked me to life, first with anger and hate, then with my love for Anna and the pain that followed, and now...now this lust that feels so wild and uncontrollable. Despite every ingrained bit of conditioning and any basic level of common sense that is screaming at me not to do it, I can't help myself. I have never felt more alive than when his lips are on me, his fingers threatening both pain and pleasure. I've never fucked a man because I wanted to, but with Nero it doesn't even feel like a choice, more like a need. But none of this changes the reality that I shouldn't even be in a professional relationship with him, let alone whatever this is. Nicholai would be so ashamed of me.

There's a soft knock at the door before it opens a crack. Nero walks in the room, wearing only a loose-fitting pair of tracksuit bottoms. His hair is wet from the shower, the strands swept back haphazardly.

"You'll need these." He holds up some bandages and approaches the bed. I sit up, crossing my legs as he takes a seat on the edge of the mattress. Reaching for me, he wraps his fingers around my wrist, pulling my hand towards him. A small frown line sinks between his eyebrows as he focuses on my hands, bandaging my ripped knuckles with strong but gentle hands. The gesture seems so at odds with everything he is. Bruises are already blossoming across his jaw in varying shades of purple.

"You should put some ice on your face."

His lips curl at one side, but his gaze never wavers from my hands. "That would just spoil your handiwork." When he's finished, he stands up and leaves. Just like that. I don't pretend to have a clue when it comes to…these things, but I've never been so confused. Perhaps we're just pretending that didn't happen.

15

UNA

O'Malley's is an Irish bar in Woodlawn. The outside has tinted windows with dark green paint peeling off the frames and an old steel door that looks like it's seen better days. If I didn't already know that it was the epicenter of the New York Irish Mafia, I might have guessed. Although, right now, Tommy and I are just ignorant tourists stopping by an authentic Irish bar. When we step inside, I can practically feel how nervous Tommy is. I persuaded him to bring me here after Nero left early this morning. He wasn't keen and I know Nero would probably lose it if he knew we were here, but he asked me to do a job, and this is me doing it.

The guys sitting at the bar turn, eyeing us as we step inside. I flash them a grin and they slowly focus their attention on me. Tommy looks Irish, but I don't want them looking too closely. If there's one thing to be said for mafia it's that everyone knows everyone else, and someone of Tommy's heritage will undoubtedly be memorable.

The barman braces his hands on the edge of the thick mahogany bar, a frown pulling his eyebrows together.

"Hi. Can I get a vodka on the rocks and a whisky?" I want them to think we're just two punters that have walked in off the street. Not that this place exactly attracts the average passer-by.

The man grunts some form of response before turning away and grabbing glasses.

"Ah, don't mind him, darlin'," one of the guys says in a thick Irish accent, flashing me a wink. He's a guy in his thirties maybe, with dirty blond hair and blue eyes that dance with humour. "Wouldn't know a good woman if she were to slap him upside the head. And you…" He flicks his eyes down my body, straightening the shirt of his collar with a cocky grin. "…are a mighty fine looking gal."

Slipping on the mask of a nice normal girl is as easy as putting on a jacket. Smiling, I lean my elbow on the bar. "My father always said, never trust an Irish boy."

"Ah, and why's that?"

"Because you'd charm the birds out of the sky," I reply, cocking a brow.

"Aye!" His friend laughs beside him, slapping him on the back. "This one would charm the knickers off a gal in a heartbeat."

The barman puts the drinks on the bar, and I hand him some money before turning away. "Nice talking to you." There's raucous laughter as I turn my back and it's decidedly less tense than when we walked in. We sit at a table in the corner, and I position myself with my back to the wall.

"I don't like this shit," Tommy grumbles, taking a heavy gulp of the whisky.

I sigh. "Keep your panties on. We'll sit. We'll drink. I'll go to the bathroom in a bit and scout an exit. Then we can go." I want to hit O'Hara here, because it's the last place he would expect, and the only place I know he'll come.

Tommy drums his fingers against his glass. Anyone looking at him would know, clear as day, he's agitated. I decide to speed things up and down my drink, before standing. The door at the back of the bar leads to a short passageway with ladies and gents toilets. I pass the bathroom door and follow the corridor that hooks right. Sure enough, at the end there is a fire exit, but it's locked, literally chained up and padlocked. Shit. Turning around, I freeze when I find the blond guy from the bar leaning against the wall, his arms folded over his chest and a wry smile on his face. A cigarette hangs from his fingers and he slowly brings it to his lips, narrowing his eyes as the smoke drifts up around his face.

"Ya lost?"

Shit.

I paint a smile on my lips. "I'm looking for the bathroom."

He jerks his head towards the corridor behind him. "Ya walked past it."

"Oh, thanks." I squeeze past him and he makes no effort to get out of my way. I can't work out whether he's onto me or if he's just trying to get in my pants. The second I get in the bathroom, I walk into a stall and bolt the door, bracing my back against it. The last thing I need is them taking too much notice of me. I need to come back in here when O'Hara is here, but then if this is anything to go by, I'm not going to go unnoticed regardless of whether blondie has made me or not. This is a mafia bar. They know everyone, see everything. Unless…

I open the stall and quickly wash my hands before stepping back outside. Sure enough, blondie is still in his spot, smoking his cigarette. I throw him a glance, making sure I lock eyes with him before open the door. I walk straight over to the bar.

"Do you have a pen?" I ask the barman. He hands me one, his surly scowl still firmly in place.

I grab one of the cardboard beer mats, the Guinness emblem all over it. I scrawl the number of one of my burner phones along with the name Isabelle onto the worn cardboard. I hand it to blondie's friend who watches me the entire time. "What's your friend's name?" I ask.

"Darren," he replies before taking a gulp of his beer.

I nod. "Give this to him, will you?

He chuckles, taking it from me. "I surely will, sweet thing."

I walk away and Tommy follows me to the exit. "What the fuck was that?" he hisses once we're outside.

"My in." We walk down the street, away from the bar.

"Nero's going to kill me."

"Nero wants O'Hara dead. He can suck it up."

16
─────

NERO

I meet Gio at the docks and stand on the wharf, watching as police swarm around a shipment on dock twelve. The sun is starting to set and they're rigging up flood lighting to work by. It's a massive shipping container and admittedly, they could be looking for anything, but I don't believe in coincidences. They're settling in for a long night, and I have two hundred grand in cocaine coming in on that boat. It's just a matter of time before they find it. I'm out of pocket, there's no coke to go onto the streets, no revenue for me to send to the cartel. I want to know who the fuck ratted me out.

"Call Tommy, tell him to speak to his contacts at the precinct. I want to know where they got a tip-off."

Gio walks away from me, phone already in hand. Meanwhile, I call Jackson because I'm pretty sure I know exactly who it is. "Boss."

.   .   .

"I HAVE A JOB FOR YOU..."

———

As soon as I step into my apartment, I see George sitting down right outside the gym. When I open the door, I'm greeted with Tommy's cry of pain followed by Una's laugh. She's on the floor and he's on top of her, his hands braced on either side of her small body. He's topless and she's wearing workout pants and a top that exposes her stomach. It would look intimate if she didn't have one leg looped around the back of his neck and her hand wrapped around her ankle, choking him out. Although, he doesn't look entirely upset with her crotch in his face.

"TAP OUT!" she shouts. His face has turned red and any minute now he's going to pass out. "Aw, Tommy." She ruffles his hair with her free hand as he loses consciousness. I've been trying to call him all damn day and he hasn't answered, and now I find him here, all over Una. She collapses back on the floor, her chest heaving as Tommy's limp body rests over her. My fuse is already burnt out today and the way her thighs are wrapped around him, his bare skin against hers... It has something hot and fast tearing through me. An irrational rage grips me, and I'm ready to shoot the fucker.

"I THOUGHT you didn't like being touched?" Even I can hear the accusing note in my voice.

.   .   .

HER EYES SNAP open and she lifts her head. "I don't."

MOVING FORWARD, I kick Tommy's unconscious body to the side. She lies on the floor while I stand over her, staring at her exposed stomach, the swell of her breasts in that skimpy top. I clench and release my fists, wanting to fuck her and fight her, preferably at the same time.

"LOOKS LIKE IT." She glares back at me, lips pressing together in a tight line.

TOMMY GROANS and slowly sits up, clutching his neck. "Fuck, Una, that hurts." She hops to her feet and shrugs, flashing him a wink and a genuine smile. Again, I don't like it.

I GRAB him by the scruff of his neck and drag him to his feet. "Where the hell have you been all day, Tommy, huh?"

HIS EYES GO WIDE and his face drains of all colour. "I...uh, here, boss."

"I CALLED YOU TEN FUCKING TIMES." I shove him away before I pound my fists into his face. I want to destroy everything in my damn path right now because I lost. Someone got one up on me. "Call the cops. I want to know who tipped them off about my shipment." He nods quickly. This is the one job I entrust to him, handle the cops, know what they know. He can be their best fucking friend for all I care as long as he gets me what I want, when I damn well want it. "Now get out," I snap. He rubs his hand over his neck, staggering towards the door. "And, Tommy… Don't touch her again." He nods and hurries away.

"WHAT THE FUCK?" Una glares at me. When I don't answer, she rolls her eyes and walks out. When I step out, Tommy is lingering just outside the door pulling his shirt on. Una is heading towards the living area.

"SORRY, BOSS. I DIDN'T REALIZE…" He trails off. "I mean, it's not…I just let her kick my ass, that's all."

"STOP TALKING. Do what I pay you for."

17

UNA

I strip out of my workout pants, throwing them in the corner angrily. He's jealous. When the hell did we get into any kind of territory where jealousy was a factor? What is this, the middle ages? And Tommy, really? Shit. I go into the bathroom and start the shower. Gripping the edge of the sink I lean over it, trying to calm my erratic pulse as I wait for the water to become red hot. When I look up, I make out a dark figure in the foggy reflection of the mirror and turn around. Nero leans against the door-frame, his thick arms folded over his chest and a scowl on his face.

"Get out."

He completely ignores me, moving closer. "No." His body presses against mine, backing me into the counter. He towers over me, the soft material of his shirt brushing against my bare stomach as his fingers wrap around my jaw. His eyes are dark and turbulent, the threat lurking just beneath the surface. Tension radiates off him in waves that has my heart skittering in my chest like a startled animal.

His mood is pitch-black tonight and I'd be lying if I said it didn't scare me.

"You don't let Tommy touch you." The low rumble of his chest vibrates against me.

I shove at him but he doesn't budge. "You're seriously jealous? You realize that's totally irrational?" He says nothing, and I shake my head. "Fuck you, Nero."

"Gladly, but I don't share, Morte."

"I'm not yours *to* share."

"You don't think so? Too bad."

His hand slips from my face, wrapping around the back of my neck before he slams his lips over mine. I rake my nails down the side of his neck and attempt to bring my knee up between his legs, but it does nothing. A low laugh rumbles against my lips before his teeth skim my bottom lip and his tongue demands entrance. My lips part and his tongue lashing against mine is nothing short of an assault. This isn't a kiss, it's a statement. I don't know how he can make me want to fuck him and slit his throat all in the same breath. That fog descends until all I can think of, feel, smell is him. He's toxic in the most addictive way. Releasing my jaw, he trails his fingers up my back, reaching for the clasp of my bra. With the briefest flick of his wrist, it comes loose and he drops his face to my chest. I gasp when his teeth clamp around my nipple, my fingers flying to his hair, needing more of his warm mouth on me. He works a burning trail down my sides until he's grabbing the material of my panties and sliding them over my thighs. A small voice in my head screams at me to stop this, but he renders me so weak. Gripping my waist, he lifts me onto the counter, and teeth sink into my neck as he wrenches my thighs apart. Tremors rip over my skin as I watch him watching me, those dark eyes igniting as he drags them over my naked body. He's still fully clothed, and I reach for the buttons of his shirt but he grips my wrist, pushing it away.

"I want to watch you shatter, Morte." I can see his dick tenting his pants from here, and yet he still makes no move to get undressed. Lips brush over my cheek before he pinches my jaw between his teeth. "I want to taste your tight little pussy." And then he drops to his knees in front of me, spreading my legs wide until my pussy is completely on display for him. A pained groan escapes his throat before he buries his face between my legs. My mouth falls open on a silent scream, and I grip his hair, pulling him closer. His hot tongue lashes across my clit; every nerve feeling like it's being electrocuted. His fingers dig into my thighs, holding me open to him, exposed. I can't feel anything but that exact pinpoint of pressure where his tongue meets me, and the hard scratch of his stubble against the soft skin of my inner thighs. Within seconds he has me moaning and writhing, rolling my hips against his face and begging him for something, anything. And then he stops.

"Look at me," he rumbles.

I drop my eyes to his, panting heavily as I watch him drag his tongue slowly up the length of my pussy. Oh god.

"Now tell me you're mine." A twisted grin lights his expression before he pushes his tongue inside me. It's too much and yet, not enough. Teeth clamp down on my clit, and I whimper, my body trembling, right on the edge. "Say it." He blows warm breath over my sensitive flesh. I clench my jaw, refusing to say the words he wants to hear. I haven't fallen so far from grace that I'll give him that.

He huffs a laugh and pushes to his feet, gripping my face in both hands. His lips are covered in my pussy and he slams them over mine so hard that his teeth click against mine. The salty taste of myself dances along my tongue as it meets his. And then he breaks away, taking a clear step away from me. "Like I said, too bad." He narrows his eyes and feigns a smile, but I can see the tension around his eyes. It mimics my own. I refuse to renege, even if my pussy is throbbing and my entire body feels like it might explode. He turns and walks out of the bathroom. Asshole.

I MAKE a clear attempt to avoid Nero for the rest of the evening. Not that it's hard; he's been in his office ever since I got out of the shower. This situation has flipped in what feels like the blink of an eye. I went from the girl he was blackmailing to the girl he fucked and now, apparently, he thinks he has some kind of claim on me. Perhaps he does. I know I could never feel this unhinged for anyone but him. Nero Verdi is a rule unto himself, a complete anomaly to everything. He doesn't need to know that though. I've already exposed too many weaknesses to him; I won't give him any more.

I steal one of his shirts because I've run out of clean clothes and apparently he has no washing machine. Figures. Not like he's going to wash his own clothes. I hope it pisses him off, and then I hope he does something about it. Oh, how I'd love to make him bleed right now. Grabbing my laptop, I go to the living room, taking a seat on the uncomfortable couch. I throw myself into work, devising my plan to take out the three Italians on his list in the space of just one week. This situation with Nero is hurtling into dangerous territory very quickly. I'm losing control and I need to get this done and get out before I completely lose all semblance of sanity. I'm staring at my laptop screen when my phone rings. Not my normal phone, my burner.

I answer it. "Hello."

"Isabelle." That Irish lilt practically sings my false name.

"Darren. I thought you'd never call."

"Ah, but ya know, good things come to those who wait." I force a girly giggle.

"I'd rather you didn't make me wait. I'm free Friday night, take me out." It's forward, and normally I'd wait for him to make the moves but I'm winging it big time, and I set a precedent when I left him my number. I can only hope he appreciates forward.

He laughs. "Friday night isn't good, sweetheart."

I tut at the same time Nero walks in the room, leaning against the doorframe with his arms folded over his chest. A deep frown line is carved between his eyebrows making his expression hard and threatening. I stare him straight in the eye and smile smugly. "Shame. I'm not the kind of girl who likes to wait," I purr way too seductively.

He pauses. "I have this thing, but I could swing something before. Drinks?"

Good enough. "Perfect. I can't wait." I hang up.

"Who was that?" His voice is tight, layered with restraint. My eyes brush over his bare chest, and I have no doubt that's a deliberate move.

I glance back at my laptop and shrug. "A job."

"My job is the only one you need to worry about."

I slowly lift my gaze to him and cock a brow. "Your job is temporary, and once it's done, I will move on, and I will go back to doing exactly what I did before I ever heard your name, Nero Verdi." I say the words coldly, driving home the fact that he doesn't own me, and he never will. "But I do have a plan that will get it done."

He slowly moves across the room and halts in front me, his legs slightly spread and his shoulders squared as he stares down at me sitting on the couch. He's wearing only a pair of workout pants, his hands shoved deep within the pockets, making him seem deceptively casual, despite his intimidating stance. He really needs to give up on that shit with me.

Smiling, I lean back into the sofa cushions, crossing one leg over the other. His eyes tighten ever so slightly and the muscle in his jaw pulses as he traces the length of my bare legs, stopping where his over-sized T-shirt sits at mid-thigh.

"Well, you said you have a plan," he says, his voice demanding and impatient.

I sigh and make a deliberate effort to check my nail polish. "I do."

After a few seconds he growls, actually growls. "I don't have time for bullshit, Morte."

I glare at him. "Well, I've got nothing but time, seeing as I'm locked in this apartment." The truth is, I just like him angry. It's when Nero's at his best, his most exciting.

A breath hisses through his teeth, and I know I'm walking a fine line. Good. He removes his hands from his pockets and leans forward, gripping the back of the couch either side of me. Those dark eyes of his meet mine, his face barely an inch away. "Fucking talk." Pressing my fingers against his mouth, I push him away from me. His lips twitch under my touch and he nips at my fingertips. I yank my hand away and his teeth snap together. "Talk."

"I told you, I can't hit them all. Even if I take Finnegan separately, three kills in one network is too much. I can't do it."

His brows pull together and his face moves even closer to mine. "We had a deal," he barely breathes against my lips.

"I didn't say I wouldn't hold up my end," I snap. "But these guys aren't just any soldiers, Nero. Capos, enforcers, they travel in herds, armed herds."

"You're *bacio della morte*." His tongue caresses the words eloquently. "I wouldn't have sought the best if it was an easy job."

"Think about it, we'll get away with one. Two? Possibly, but the third is going to get spooked. Each one I hit makes the next harder. Surprise is my forte. I'll lose it."

He finally pushes away from me and sits on the edge of the coffee table opposite me, his thighs spread and elbows resting on them. Absently, he swipes his thumb back and forth over his bottom lip. "What do you suggest?"

"Call a truce."

His eyebrows shoot up. "A truce?" He laughs incredulously.

"Call a meeting. Get them all in one room. I'll do the rest."

He laughs again and shakes his head. "They won't fall for it."

"Why not?"

"Ah, Morte. Anyone in the mafia, anyone who knows me, or has even heard my name will know..." He tilts his head to the side and a wicked streak flashes across his eyes. "I don't make peace, I make war. I don't call truces when I can spill blood instead." A small tremor works over my skin and my stomach tightens at his words. I've known men like him my whole life and yet, there is no one like him. He's so utterly feral, so merciless. His arrogance annoys me; his manipulation infuriates me, even though I'd do exactly the same if I were him. His savagery excites me, and his blood lust sings to me. The monster that he is calls to the one that I keep chained up, released only when I kill, but even then, leashed, restricted to clean kills and professional pride. Nero would paint this city red and set a throne from which to survey his blood-stained empire on the mountain of bodies. He wants power and he doesn't care how he gets it. He's right; no one would believe he wants peace, but of course there are two sides to Nero. There's the feral side that wants to bathe in blood, and then there's the sophisticated front he wears so easily. If faced with that side of him, they may just believe he's stepping up to his newfound responsibilities.

"Go to them as the capo. Pretend you have the collective interests at heart and that you're prepared to put aside differences for the greater good." He scowls at me as if the words offend him, and I roll my eyes. "Throw a few threats in there if you feel the need to get your dick out. You're Nero Verdi." I raise a pointed eyebrow. "You want power? Take. It."

"Ah, Morte, you should know better than anyone, I always take what I want." His eyes drop to my mouth as though pointing out that is what he wants right now. "And what will you do if I get them there?"

"Kill them all, of course. But first, we go after Finnegan."

He shakes his head. "We can't hit Finnegan tomorrow. The situation's changed."

"Changed how? We aren't going to get another chance any time soon."

He stares me down. "I said no."

"If he leaves the country, I'm not waiting weeks to hit him again, sitting here while you find every excuse not to get Anna."

"Not. Tomorrow," he growls.

Biting back a retort, I stand, needing to walk away from him. He might not be going after Finnegan but he doesn't know that I already have an in. I need this to happen. I need to finish this job and get Anna. What Nero does, I don't care.

18

UNA

My watch reads seven thirty. I said I'd meet Darren at eight. Tommy is sitting across the table from me playing solitaire while I pretend to be doing something constructive on my laptop. I've barely seen Nero for the last two days, and I get the impression he's tied up in mafia shit. He's permanently snappy, drinking like a fish and spending almost all of his time in the office. I don't care. While he's focused on other things, he's leaving me alone, which is good.

Wordlessly, I get up and head to my room. When I arrived here there were already some clothes in the walk-in closet. All of them are brand new with the tags still on. I pick out a simple black dress. God knows what he thought I would possibly need this for, but it's coming in handy now. I managed to order a pair of shoes online, and Tommy, of course, opened the package because I'm untrustworthy and likely to get bombs posted to the apartment or something. When he saw the shoes, he looked so confused. I explained that all girls like shoes and of course he just believed me, bless him. Slipping on the dress and the shoes, I check my face in the mirror, adding a layer of blood-red lipstick and dragging my fingers through my long white-blonde hair.

Tommy immediately looks up when he hears the click of heels on the kitchen floor. His eyebrows shoot up so far they're practically touching his hairline. "Uh, wow. You… you look amazing, but why are you dressed like that?"

With a smile, I pull the gun from behind my back. His eyes pop wide and he barely has time to try and scramble from the barstool before I bring the butt down hard on this temple. His eyes roll back and he goes down hard. I feel bad, but this is necessary. Nero wants to dictate how this job goes down but that wasn't part of this agreement. He hired me to do a job, and I'm going to get it done. For all of his bullshit saying we're in this together, we're not. As usual, it's me against the world.

I put the 9mm pistol in my handbag and swipe the key card out of Tommy's pocket before finding a pen and paper and scrawling a note to Nero. He's going to be so angry. The thought makes me smile.

DARREN IS SITTING at the bar when I get to the place he wanted to meet. It's a new bar a few streets over from O'Malley's. The décor is all brushed steel and slate floors, very industrial. I hop up on the stool next to him.

"Is the vodka any good here?"

He turns to face me and his eyes immediately sweep the length of my body appreciatively, a slow smile pulling at his lips. "You look stunning. And I wouldn't know, I'm a whisky man." He's wearing fitted jeans and a grey shirt with no tie. Darren Derham – yes, I looked him up – is a good-looking guy. But he's also pretty high in the Irish mob on this side of the city. He works closely with Brandon O'Kieffe who's the capo equivalent in these parts. If I can get an in with Darren it's unlikely it will be questioned, but his position also means he's intelligent, cautious and anything but naïve. The benefit of being a woman is even the shrewdest of men never suspect anything, after all, how much harm could a girl possibly do? He orders me a vodka and the barman slides the drink in front of me. The ice clinks against the glass and he studies me as I lift it to my lips, taking a heavy swallow.

"So, Isabelle, what brings you to New York?"

I tilt my head to the side. It's a simple enough question, and yet…

"How do you know I'm not *from* New York?" I ask, adding a seductive smile to make sure it doesn't come off as defensive.

"The accent." He lifts his chin and picks up his whisky glass. "You're not American." Shit, he's good. I barely have any accent at all and you have to pay close attention to pick it up. All my instincts are telling me that I'm made, but I push them down. All I can think about is that I need to get this done. Nero makes me lose focus, but the fact is, I'm locked in that apartment, working for him in exchange for Anna, no other reason. And after his little pissing contest the other night, I don't trust his motivations anymore. No, I have my in. I'm going to see it through. It's a measured risk, for Anna.

So, I smile and feign an offended expression. "And there was me thinking that I'd mastered the New York accent."

He laughs. "Almost."

"Well, I'm just here for work," I tell him.

He nods. "Where in Russia are you from?"

I can feel my expression tightening with strain but I

fight it, playing my role perfectly. "Moscow. My father was a lawyer there," I lie easily. "But I always wanted to come to America. Now, *you* can't even pretend to be from here," I tease.

He braces his elbows on the bar and smiles at me. "Dublin, born and bred. I came here for work, too." He downs the rest of his drink. The irony is not lost on me, two people in a normal bar, looking normal, pretending to *be* normal and trying their utmost to convince the other that they are indeed normal, yet he's in the mafia and I'm a hired killer.

We sit, both continuing our façade and exchanging pleasant conversation. We tell each other about the people we aren't, the people we might have been, I suppose. Slowly, I shift closer to him and when I place my hand on his thigh, he barely acknowledges it, comfortable with my touch. His hand lands over mine on his thigh and he leans into me, his lips so close I'm sure he's going to kiss me, but then his phone rings. He releases a frustrated breath and pulls away to pick it up. I quietly sip on my drink while he talks to whoever is on the other end. Now, Irish is English essentially, until two Irish people talk to each other and then it's just noise. I can't make out a word he's saying. He eventually hangs up and when he turns to face me again, I flash him a wide smile.

"I have to go." He sighs, and he doesn't look too happy about it.

I paint a disappointed expression on my face. "Oh, okay."

He stares at me for a long while and then pushes to his feet, pressing his body against my knees and running his knuckles over my jaw. The touch makes me uncomfortable. "I wish I could bring you with me, but unless you like a bar full of pervy Irishmen, I can't imagine it's your scene."

I shrug. "I happen to like pervy Irishmen."

He laughs. "I'll take that as a compliment." He drags his eyes over my body again. "Fine. But you asked for it."

Well, that was easier than I anticipated. Now, the next bit is considerably harder.

O'Malley's is packed tonight. Guys are hanging over the bar, drinking and laughing. Music blares from the jukebox and if I didn't know what this place is, the nature of these people, then it could be any local bar on a Friday night. Everyone smiles at Darren and some clap him on the back. Curious glances are thrown my way, but they last only a few seconds. There are a few women in here; most of them sprawled across one lap or another. Clutching my handbag close to me, I wish that I could have my gun in hand, ready. These are not the kinds of situations I put myself in. I plan and avoid unnecessary risks. Someone taps me on the shoulder, and I turn around. In the next second someone grabs my wrist, their grip too tight to be friendly. I tamper down my more volatile instincts and my eyes dart around, looking for Darren. He's gone.

"You're new," a voice says, quietly from behind me.

I glance over my shoulder at the dark-haired guy who is only inches away from me before looking at the guy to my left, the one with his hand clamped around my wrist. "You're hurting me," I whimper pathetically.

The guy behind me laughs. "If you'll kindly follow me." He passes me, yanking my bag from my grasp, before I'm pushed to follow him. This right here is why you don't go off half-cocked. Damn it.

———

I'M handcuffed to a chair and the dark-haired guy is pacing in front of me. Finnegan O'Hara. He must be in his forties, the salt and pepper of his beard and crow's-feet at his eyes the only sign of aging. He's a big guy, broad-shouldered and thick-set with an air about him that suggests he's capable of far more than just handling shipments. Two of his guys are on the door, the only exit, and there aren't even any windows in here. The floor beneath my feet is rough stone and the walls are concrete, reminding me of the facility I trained in, the Russian fortress buried in the snow. Both walls are lined with barrels and it smells like old beer; the cellar of the bar. I still don't know why they've brought me down here, so I'll play the frightened woman until they play their hand. A steady stream of tears flow down my face and my chest shudders with each breath. Men, even the hardest of them, don't like having to deal with emotional women and they will subtly focus their attention elsewhere to avoid having to deal with it. So, while his men stare straight ahead and he glances at the floor, I manage to drop the small silver blade from the cuff at my wrist into my hand. This bracelet may well be the most valuable thing I own. It's not an easy job, but I manage to get the end of the fine blade into the lock, wiggling it until I feel a small pop.

"Do you know who I am?" Finnegan asks, his expression serious.

"No." I shake my head. "Please let me go," I sob.

He huffs a laugh before turning on me and leaning over, gripping my forearms. I grind my teeth together, trying not to show my discomfort. "I know exactly who you are, Una Ivanov." My face goes blank and the tears cut off, my breathing returning to normal. There's only so much acting I can do. I've been made.

"How do you know my name?"

His lips twitch, and I hate that I'm on the back foot. I'm never vulnerable, but right now he has me on the ropes. "Nero Verdi has a reputation, but I have the contacts in this city," he drawls, his Irish accent more prevalent than Darren's. I narrow my eyes and say nothing. This is a leak on Nero's side. Fuck. "And my contacts are loyal to me. They trust me to protect them."

"If you know who I am, then you know what the cost of killing me is." I cock a brow, and I don't have to say a damn thing. When I said I was immune, I wasn't kidding. Am I an assassin? Yes. Am I technically fair game? Of course. But, and this is a very big but, I am like a daughter to Nicholai Ivanov. The mafias, for the most part, try and remain amicable and maintain peace where they can but the Russians...well, we're hot-headed by nature. No one wants a war with Nicholai. I've seen what he's capable of and he can make Nero look like Santa Claus.

He pushes away and takes a packet of cigarettes out of his pocket, pulling one loose and placing it between his lips. He lights it and stands a few feet away from me, blowing a long stream of smoke through his nose. "I have no fight with you or that mad Russian fuck." He spits on the ground. "But I have a fight with Nero Verdi and apparently, he's hired your services, so I have a job for you, Miss Ivanov. I want you to kill Nero Verdi for me. He won't even see it coming."

Oh, how the tables turn.

19

NERO

My eyes land on Tommy's prone body the second the elevator doors open. I tuck behind the small protruding wall that divides the foyer from the kitchen and feel around underneath the side table next to the gym door. My fingers brush over the gun that's taped to the underside, and I yank it loose. George and Zeus run up to me excitedly, and I relax. If there were someone in the apartment still, then they'd let me know. It's why I have them. Going to Tommy, I crouch down, pressing my finger to his neck. He's fine, just unconscious. A nasty red mark is blossoming across his temple and it looks like he got pistol-whipped badly. I shake his shoulder and he groans, eyelids twitching before they finally open.

"Boss?"

I sigh. "Where's Una?" I know, without even having to ask, exactly where she's gone, but I want to hear him say the words. I want him to tell me that he let her fucking go.

"She, uh, she knocked me out," he says, dropping his eyes away from my scrutinizing stare.

I push to my feet. "Where is she?"

"I don't know."

"Fuck!" I brace my hands against the kitchen island and it's then that I notice the scrap of paper in the middle. Picking it up, I read over the scrawled words.

Nero.

Don't get your panties in a wad. I've gone to do my job. Don't wait up.

Una.

O'Hara. She's gone after fucking O'Hara, and he knows she's coming. Shit!

"What time did she leave?"

"About eight."

It's ten thirty.

I drop my head forward. "She's gone after O'Hara. Two hours is too long and he knows she's coming. She's probably dead." I say the words calmly, but I don't feel calm. I feel…aggravated, to the point that I want to rip this place apart.

"She might not be. She…I mean…" he stammers.

I twist my gaze towards him. "She what?"

He takes a seat across from me, resting his head in his hands. "She has this guy, Darren."

"You need to talk really fucking fast, Tommy," I growl.

"Look, she made me take her to O'Malley's on Tuesday," he says in a rush. "This guy tried to talk to her, so she gave him her number. She was going to use him as an in to get to O'Hara."

"Do you know any more about this guy?"

"Derham, I think she said his name was Darren Derham."

Well, this just gets better and better. "Find me details. I want family, a wife, a mother, anything you can find." I pick up my keys and take another gun out of the kitchen drawer. "I will deal with you later." That woman is incapable of listening to anything I say and now she's dragging Tommy into this shit with her. And me? I'm running head-first after her for reasons I can't begin to explain even to myself.

———

JACKSON PULLS UP in the alleyway just around the corner from O'Malley's. I called him on my way over because I sure as hell need backup and when it comes to fighting, Jackson's always handy. He gets out of the black SUV and eyes me with a tight expression before opening the back door. Moving beside him, I stare at the woman on the back seat, her stomach swollen and her face streaked with tears.

"I have no desire to hurt you. Call Darren. Now. Tell him where you are and that if he doesn't come alone, I'm going to kill you." A ragged sob comes from her. Fuck me, I don't have time for this shit. Jackson hands her a phone and she takes it, hands shaking as she follows my instructions.

"Darren!" she cries, her voice breaking. She draws several heaving breaths, tears and snot running down her face. "I'm in the alley one block over from the bar. He... he's going to kill me."

Snatching the phone away from her, I put it to my ear. The sound of dull music is in the background, as if he's in a hallway or a side room away from the main bar. "You have something I want, Mr. Derham. So, you are going to come and meet me, alone, or I am going to blow your pretty little girlfriend's brains all over the dirty fucking street." My voice rises and then I hang up, tossing the phone to Jackson.

"Point a gun at her head. You see any more than one guy walk around that corner, shoot her."

"Oh god." She starts whimpering and crying before she clasps her hands together and starts praying under her breath. I have no sympathy for that shit, and you know why? Because if you get involved with a mafia guy, this is to be expected. And if she didn't know he was mafia... well, that just makes her stupid. The mafia are all about protecting women and keeping them out of it, they create these rules that make them untouchable, rely on honor, and it works...until a bastard like me comes along. I don't have any honor and I'll use any means necessary to get what I want. If he wants to take what's mine, he can be damn sure I'll take what's his.

A few minutes later, a figure appears at the mouth of the alley. He's alone but his fingers are wrapped around a gun. "Who the fuck are you?" he asks, his voice strained.

"I'm the guy with a gun to your woman's head." I point towards Jackson who has his gun trained on the back seat.

"Darren!" she screams, and I see his eyes pinch slightly, his lips pressing together.

"What do you want?" he asks through clenched teeth.

I approach him and place my gun under his chin. He stares me straight in the eye. "I want Una."

"She'll already be dead."

I ram the barrel of the gun into his throat hard enough to make him gag and choke.

"You had best hope not, because at this point, her life is tied to dear Polly's here."

"O'Hara has her," he says through clenched teeth.

"Where?"

"The cellar of the bar."

"Thank you. You've been very helpful." I pull the trigger and a bloody gaping hole appears in his throat. He's seen Una's face, knows who she is. He's a liability.

The girl starts screaming and it's loud enough to wake the dead. Jackson leans in the back of the car and then it's silent. He closes the door and opens the trunk, handing me a semi-automatic.

"Grab his feet." I pick up Darren's shoulders and Jackson gets his ankles. I don't have time to fix this now, so we just throw him in the trunk.

Only one guy guards the back of the bar. We duck down in the shadows behind a dumpster and watch for a second.

"Boss, we're walking into the Irish stronghold," Jackson says. I don't respond because I'm well aware. "Is she really worth getting killed for?"

Is she? I don't know. All I know is I want her back. I'm not ready for my vicious little butterfly to meet her end. If anyone is going to kill her, it will be me.

"We'll see, won't we?" I push to my feet. The guard turns to face us and Jackson shoots him, the muted pop from the silencer the only sound before he hits the ground. I'm hoping that they're all too drunk to pay too much attention and honestly, he's right, this is their stronghold. It's the last place they would expect a hit.

I fire off one round at the lock, yanking the old door open. I have no idea what I'm walking into, and I'm not sure I care.

20

UNA

"I don't work for free, Mr O'Hara. And honestly, I expect a certain level of professional courtesy."

He laughs. "I'm showing you it by not killing you."

I narrow my eyes, lounging in the chair casually. "Haven't you heard? I'm untouchable."

He moves closer. "No one is untouchable. So what will it be? You work for me or I use you and torture information out of you."

I throw my head back and laugh. "You'd be wasting your time." I spring up from the chair, taking him by surprise as I clasp the curved metal of the handcuff and rake the serrated edge over his neck. He staggers back a step, and I get a clear line of sight to the guard on the left of the door. I throw the slim blade in my other hand at said guard and it hits him in the side of the neck. Blood spurts from the small nick like a hosepipe being turned on. The other guard glances at his friend before pointing his gun at me, but I duck behind his boss who provides an ample body shield. Of course, O'Hara has recovered from my earlier swipe. It was only a flesh wound and although there's a lot of blood, he's annoyingly fine. The door flies open on a bang and the quick *pop pop* of silenced gunfire has Finnegan grabbing a handful of my hair and turning us to face the door. He forces me in front of him, ramming the barrel of his gun into the side of my neck.

"Nero." I barely breathe. He stands in the doorway looking like the devil himself come to mete out his wrath. His chest rises and falls raggedly and the muscles in his jaw pulse beneath the skin. Jackson lingers in the hallway just behind him. His gaze briefly touching on mine before he goes back to keeping watch.

"Well, well. I see ya finally found the balls to come after me yourself." O'Hara taunts, pulling my hair harder.

Nero tilts his head to the side slightly. "Oh, no. This one's all on Una," he says casually, but the meaning is all too clear, this is my fault.

"I can see why you'd want her back." O'Hara presses his face into my hair and sniffs. I scowl and try to shrug him off. "But this is a risk. Isn't that her job?"

Nero's gaze meets mine, dark and turbulent and promising nothing but pain and retribution. Something passes between us, a mutual understanding of necessary violence. Anyone else might hesitate, but I see the minute twitch of the muscle in his shoulder before he pulls the gun up. Grabbing O'Hara's right wrist, I shove it away from me, digging my finger hard into the nerve that runs through his forearm. I twist my body side-on as I do. Two bangs ring out, and then he's falling. O'Hara lands flat on his back, gasping desperately for air as a red stain slowly bleeds out across the centre of his chest. Nero comes to stand beside me and fires one shot at the dying man's head. He wordlessly walks straight out of the room. There is no time to hang around, so I follow him, and Jackson falls in behind me. I can practically see the anger swirling around Nero. For once though, it's warranted. I've always been meticulous and know that mistakes and rash action are what get you caught. Acting out of desperation could have gotten me killed. And Nero...I'm supposed to be taking out his target's so he's not associated with it, so why come after me? He's just implicated himself and for what? To play the white knight?

We walk a block over before he turns into a dark alley-way. A black SUV and the Maserati are parked under the cover of darkness. "Get in the car," he says without looking at me. He makes me feel like a chastised child, so on pure principle, I lean against the back of the car and cross my arms over my chest.

"Take the girl to the hospital," he says to Jackson. What girl? "And get rid of him."

Nero grabs my arm and shoves me towards the passenger side of the car. "Do not fucking push me right now, Una." His voice is a low rumble, rolling thunder that signals a storm is about to hit. He shoves me in the car and gets in, wheels spinning past the SUV as he pulls out of the alley. The tension in the car wraps around, pressing on my chest until it's stifling. His anger is a palpable thing, and his silence is ominous to say the least.

By the time he pulls into the parking garage at the apartment, I can't wait to get out of the car. I don't partic-ularly want to be in another confined space with him, but I follow him to the elevator and get in.

When I can't take it anymore, I glance sideways at him. "Are you going to say anything?" I ask.

He cracks his neck to the side and tilts his head back, jaw flexing over and over. "You're lucky I didn't shoot you myself."

"I thought –"

He shoves me back into the elevator wall and slams his fists against the metal beside my head with a loud bang. "You don't get to fucking think," he hisses, blowing hot angry breath over my face. My heart pounds in my chest so hard it's all I can hear. I squeeze my eyes shut and swallow heavily. "You disobeyed me."

My own temper spikes. "I'm not one of your soldiers, Nero. You asked me to do a job. How I do it was not part of the agreement."

He grips my throat the same way he always does when he's mad. "He knew you were coming, and you better believe he would have killed you." The elevator pings and the doors open but neither of us move.

"Those are the risks of the job."

His hand physically trembles against my neck before he shoves away from me and turns his back.

"Damn it, Una." He drags both hands through his hair. I walk straight past him and feel him following me. "I hired you because you're the best. This shit…this is not the best."

I turn on him, jabbing my finger into the center of his chest. "You didn't hire me! You blackmailed me. There's a difference."

His head tilts to the side and he looks at me in that way that has me taking a step back. Of course, he follows. "So, what? You feel slighted so you rush headfirst into a bullet between the eyes?"

"No, I…" I keep moving backwards with him stalking me. "Why do you even care? I didn't compromise you. He already knew it was you." My back hits the kitchen island and he places his hands on either side of me, gripping the edge. "Why do you care?" I repeat. I need to know, because right now, I'm freefalling through the unknown and my stupid little heart is hoping he'll catch me, determined that there must be a reason why he saved me. Meanwhile, my head says he'll stand and watch me hit the ground and smile as my body breaks and shatters in front of him.

He leans in until his lips are brushing so close to my face, his breath caressing my lips as he speaks. "I told you, Morte, you're mine." Then his lips crash against mine. He kisses me like he wants to crawl inside me and consume me, and I let him, because his possession, his brutal need... I want it. No one has ever risked a damn thing for me before, but I know he risked his life coming for me. In his own warped and depraved way, he cares. No one has truly cared about me since I was eight years old. I never knew I wanted or needed it until this exact second. Nero makes me feel safe and the realization shocks me to my core, because he's anything but safe. I don't need protection and I sure as hell don't need a white knight, but I want this savage creature. I want his complete lack of morals, his violence and his need for power and blood. Kissing him back, I tug at his jacket and push it past his shoulders. He shrugs out of it as his lips tear away from mine and ravage the side of my neck. I tilt my head to the side, allowing him more access.

"You make me so damn angry. I want to fuck you until you bleed," he snarls, and I shiver, my breath hitching in my throat. "And this fucking dress." He roughly grabs the skirt and shoves it up, a low groan escaping his throat when his fingers brush all the way up to my hips. I'm not wearing any underwear because the dress is skin-tight. He grips my thighs and lifts me easily. I wrap my legs around him, clinging to his broad shoulders as he moves. He slams me against the wall and one of the paintings sways danger- ously. It's nothing but hands and teeth and lips as he drives his point home. My fingers thread through his hair, pulling at the thick strands, wanting more, wanting his punishment just as much as his pleasure. He bites down on my neck hard enough that I actually feel his teeth puncture my skin. I and grab the collar of his shirt, wrenching it apart. Buttons scatter, hitting the tile like rain in a storm, an apt backing for the hurricane that is Nero. Lips slam over mine again, fighting, demanding, taking. His hot, bare skin presses against the inside of my thighs and I'm so desperate for him that I reach between us and yank at his belt buckle. I'm consumed with this unexplainably heightened need to feel him inside me, and he gives me what I want, shoving his pants and boxers over his thighs and ramming his cock inside me. It's like retribution and salvation all at once, pain and pleasure, light and dark, right and wrong...it all blends together until the lines that define us disappear and it's no longer him and me, just us. We are one and the same, the embodiment of each other, two splintered halves of the fractured whole.

His forehead presses against mine and his hand wraps around the back of my neck, holding me there, forcing me to share the same air as him. I grasp his face in both my hands and close my eyes, feeling every rough thrust of his hips, the small spike of pain that comes with having him buried so deep inside me. I listen to every feral groan and staggered breath, and I embrace it all, letting him dominate and own me for just a few precious moments.

The picture on the wall crashes to the floor, the glass smashing and flying across the tile. He only fucks me harder, pounding into me until I don't know where he ends and I begin. I throw my head back against the wall, my mouth falling open on a long moan. His lips rest against my throat, teeth touching my skin but never biting down as he groans. Everything in me tightens, and I cling to him as my body detonates, sending wave after wave of pleasure tearing through my muscles, setting fire to my nerve endings. He growls into my neck, biting down on my shoulder as he thrusts into me harder and stiffens on a long groan.. Bracing his hand against the wall beside my head, he breathes heavily against my neck. My body trembles and my heart thrums in my chest, pounding against my ribs. My fingers drift down the side of his neck as I try to catch my breath, and he pulls back, eyes meeting mine. We stare at each other, saying nothing and everything with one look. His hand grips my neck roughly.

"The next time you do something like that, I will kill you myself," he says, and I smile.

He storms away, leaving me standing there alone.

———

MY HAND SHAKES, my heart hammering in my chest so hard that my pulse thrums against my eardrums, a symphony of fear and heartbreak.

"Please," I beg, lifting my eyes to Nicholai.

His expression softens as he steps closer to me, reaching out and brushing a tendril of hair away from my face. "Become what you were meant to be, little dove." His thumb trails over my jaw, and I close my eyes as a tear slips down my cheek. "Put a bullet in his head or put a bullet in your own," he says harshly. "You cannot live with weakness. Fix it one way or another." His lips brush over the side of my face.

I lift my gaze, staring over his arm at the far wall. "Please don't make me do this," I beg. Tears blur my vision, and I don't care that I look weak.

Nicholai looks at me in disgust. "See what he does to you? You are a weapon and weapons don't weep. Make a choice."

The concrete walls of the room press in on me until I can barely breathe. Nicholai's hand slips away from my face and he steps back.

My trembling finger rests over the trigger of the gun, and I swallow heavily, hating the fact that I'm so weak. I lift my eyes to Alex, chained to the far wall. His torso is bare, covered in slices that bleed over his skin. Sweat mixes with the blood, coating the chiseled muscles of his body in a crimson glow. His dark hair is damp with sweat and a few loose tendrils fall across his face. I stare into his beautiful green eyes, so full of pain, so full of longing. Longing for what can never be. Longing for a fantasy, a dream, but dreams don't exist in this place. This is where the damned are born and created, shaped and molded until there's nothing left but the cold urge to kill, to take and destroy. I thought I'd found a brief reprieve in Alex's arms, an oasis in this warped version of hell, but I was wrong. Because there is no escape from yourself, from what you've become. Alex made me forget, for just a second. He makes me feel things that I haven't felt since I was taken, since Anna. Love. Kindness.

Meeting his gaze, I tighten the grip on the gun. His eyes are resigned, begging me, but not for reprieve. He's begging me to shoot him. "Do it, Titch." My vision blurs with tears and a sharp pain rips through my chest.

"I love you," I choke. Tears track down my cheeks and a sharp pain rips through my chest.

"Shoot him, Una!" Nicholai roars.

With a ragged cry, I lift the gun, aiming between his eyes.

"Forgive me," I whisper as I pull the trigger. His eyes go wide as the bullet rips through his skull. I scream.

21

NERO

The sound of screaming jolts me awake. On a groan, I get out of bed. The second I open my door, Una lets out another scream but it's not coming from her room, it's coming from downstairs. Descending the stairs, I find her on the couch, tossing and thrashing in her sleep. George is sitting bolt upright at the end of the couch, watching her like he's witnessing an exorcism.

"Alex!" she cries, her voice shrill and staggered. A small whimper leaves her lips and she no longer seems like a lethal killer, more like a scared little girl.

"Una." I shove her shoulder but keep my distance because I'm not a fan of what follows when she wakes up. She sits bolt upright, gasping for air as her eyes dart around the room. Her face slowly twists towards me, though I can't clearly make out her expression in the darkness.

"Why are you on the couch?" I snap. I'm tired and this exact moment is the culmination of a line of shit events.

"I..." She stammers over herself and I exhale an impatient breath before reaching for her and yanking her off the couch.

"What are you...?" Throwing her over my shoulder, she squeaks before going rigid stiff. I don't care. I carry her up the stairs and along the hallway into my room before tossing her on the bed. She grunts and bounces on the mattress, landing sprawled. She's still wearing that black dress which is hiked up her thighs, exposing miles of long, toned legs. And of course, I know she's not wearing any underwear.

I drag my eyes to her face, but she won't look at me. She pulls her knees to her chest and wraps her arms around them. I'm waiting for her to bitch and moan at me, but she doesn't. Instead, she withdraws into herself, as if I'm not even in the room. For long moments, nothing but silence reigns between us, and I can almost feel her turmoil from here. I don't care that she has nightmares, because any half sane person in her position would. You don't get to be the kiss of death without seeing and doing horrific things. After a while you'd become numb to it, acts that seemed so monstrous before slowly fade in your mind until they're just normal. Emotions that were once sharp and colorful become dull and grey. No, the nightmares are no concern of mine, but the fact that she always calls for this Alex...that concerns me. When she calls his name, she sounds so tortured.

"Who's Alex?" I ask, staring down at her.

"I told you, someone I killed."

"You've killed a lot of people, Morte, and you aren't screaming their names in your sleep. So, I'll ask again, who is he?" I don't know what it is about it that irritates me. Perhaps because this Alex seems to be the only chink in that impenetrable armor of hers besides her sister. Una doesn't have chinks, and for him to be on any kind of level with Anna, well, he must be important.

"Was. He *was* my friend," she whispers, turning her face towards me. Those indigo eyes hold mine in the darkness, so hard, so sad. "And in a way, I loved him."

"I didn't think you capable."

She turns her face away again and knots the sheets between her fingers. When I'm sure she's going to say no more, she starts talking. "I was fifteen years old and naïve. I thought I loved him, and Nicholai didn't like it, so I was forced to choose between him and myself. I chose me. Killing Alex made me what I am. Nicholai was right to do it. Alex was a weakness, it made me strong." She says the words but they're robotic, as though she's recited them to herself a hundred times.

I knew Nicholai was crazy but even by my standards that's pretty fucked up. When I first bartered her sister in exchange for the job, I threw the threat of Nicholai out there purely on a hunch, having no idea whether or not it would work. But I'd heard stories, had my suspicions.

"And that's why you're here," I say, as a piece of the cryptic puzzle that makes up Una clicks into place. "That's why you haven't found Anna, because Nicholai would kill her."

She slowly nods. "He wouldn't do it out of spite, but he would do it to keep me strong." I can tell she truly believes that. "The strong survive and the weak die, forgotten and inconsequential." She shakes her head. "She'd be better off dead anyway."

"Probably." It sounds cruel, but I won't lie to her. Anna's situation is a fate worse than death.

Her gaze snaps to mine. "She's not like us, Nero. She was good and pure. Promise me you will get her."

I move around the bed, slipping beneath the covers.

Her gaze follows me. "Technically, our deal is broken. You didn't kill O'Hara."

She drags a hand through her hair. "Promise me," she pleads. I've never seen her look so desperate. So fragile. Her wings of steel are crumpled and broken.

I sigh. "I intend to buy her. It's the only way to get a slave out of the Sinaloa." Her eyes search my face, seeking the trace of a lie. "But you broke our deal, so now I propose a new one."

"What do you want?"

"I want to know why you have such loyalty to a man who would force you to kill a boy you profess love for. Tell me and our deal stands."

She drops her chin and a lock of white hair falls over her face, shining brightly in the moonlight. "I'll tell you why if you tell me why you wanted your own brother dead."

I smile and press my finger under her chin, forcing her to look at me. "That's not the deal though, is it?" She stares at me, waiting. "Fine, Lorenzo was my half-brother. I hated his father and they both hated me."

"Why?"

"Because my mother was a whore and I was a bastard," I say quickly. "Your turn."

She squeezes her eyes closed and takes a deep breath that has her shoulders rising and falling. "My parents died when I was eight and Anna and I were in an orphanage, until my matron sold me to the bratva at thirteen. They tried to rape me, turn me into a whore, but Nicholai saved me. He said I was a fighter." She sets her jaw, and I can see the bloodlust in her eyes. I can imagine a young Una, small and scared but every bit as unbreakable as she is now. "He saved me. He taught me how to fight, gave me power." The way she says it makes it sound like some guy teaching a little girl to throw a few punches, but I know better.

"You were one of the bratva's child soldiers." She nods. It all makes so much sense now. The Russian mafia have always 'adopted' orphans and turned them into soldiers, but Nicholai Ivanov went one better. He made his own force of elite assassins. They're feared and spoken of across the world, but Una is the jewel in his crown, the favorite, the one he calls daughter. Because he saved her. Because he created her. But as the pieces fall into place, I suddenly see her for what she really is. The very qualities that make us human have been torn from her and though she is indeed strong, she's also irrevocably broken. Anna is her exception, the ghost of humanity within Una. It's her lack of humanity that draws me to her though, because we're both monsters surrounded by people. The difference between Una and me though is that she's still fighting herself, otherwise she wouldn't have nightmares. Anna is the good, the redemption that she's clinging to, and in that sense, I completely understand why Nicholai would kill her. To do so would break Una so completely that he would unleash a creature like no other. She would be perfect. "If you're so loyal to him, then where does Anna fit in?" I ask.

She shifts on the bed and lies down beside me. "Anna is my one weakness," she says simply. "But you already know that. I will do anything I have to for her, even if it means standing against Nicholai," she says fiercely. Yes, Nicholai has created a little monster but when you make one so strong, you often lose control, and I have a feeling that Nicholai's prize dog is about to bite him.

Anna maybe Una's weakness but Una is fast becoming mine. I would say it bothers me, but what's the point? She's like a disease that can't be cured, infecting me, spreading and consuming everything until I'm driven mad for her.

She's slowly fracturing me, forcing her way inside me until my very cells are forced to evolve and accommodate her, acclimating to this newfound need. She's so much more than just a warm body to stick my dick in. She's the kiss of death, and when I look at her, I see something I've never seen in anyone else; my equal. She's the only one who challenges me, and I find myself waiting for her defiance, craving it even.

For the first time in a long time, I want something other than just power. I want her. She will be *my* jewel in *my* crown. My broken queen.

———

I WAKE up to the scent of vanilla and the subtle hint of gun oil. My dick is rock hard and presses against something warm and soft. I open my eyes and tighten my arm around Una's small body. My chest is plastered to her back and her ass is just right there, cupping my cock like it was made for it. I frown because I like the feeling of waking up with her and that bothers me. We fight and fuck, and ultimately, Una is mine whether she likes it or not, but this...this is too...normal. This isn't blurring the line, it's wiping it the fuck away. No matter how I feel about her, I still need her to do a job. We are still Una and Nero, the assassin and the capo. People like us don't get normal, and I don't want it. I pull my arm away from her slowly, torn between needing to step away and wanting to sink my dick between her legs. I get out of bed and get in the shower. The warm spray washes over me and I wrap my hand around my rock-hard dick, stroking over the length and picturing Una's naked body, that look of violence she gets in her eyes when I fuck her. My muscles lock and pleasure tears through me so hard my knees go weak and I have to throw my hand out

against the shower wall. This is what she does; she almost
brings me to my knees. Almost.

When I get out of the shower, Una's gone. I answer a
couple of emails, before going downstairs. I find her sitting
at the breakfast bar sipping on coffee. She's wearing yoga
pants and her sports bra, and her body is coated in a thin
sheen of sweat, I assume from working out.

"I need your help with something this morning." I
move over to the coffee machine.

"Oh, you're letting me out?" She snorts.

I move behind her, placing my hands either side of her
body and gripping the breakfast bar. My face is level with
her neck and I can smell the subtle scent of her sweat
mixing with her shampoo. I skim my lips over her skin and
she shivers. "I'd happily tie you to the bed and leave you
there, but we were set up, and payback's a bitch." I nip at
her skin and when I pull away, a twisted smile is on her
lips.

"Yes, she is."

———

I DROP Una off and take the long drive to the Hamptons
house. I haven't been here much in the last couple of
weeks. I've left Gio running the place while I play out my
game of strategy. Gio greets me outside the front door the
second I get out of the car.

"Any problems?" I ask.

"None." He falls in step beside me as I make my way
inside the house which is alive with activity. We called in a
lot of guys after last night's shitshow. I'm just waiting for an
Irish show of retribution.

We go straight down to the basement and I shove open
the old steel door that leads into the main room, the same

room that Una watched me set fire to someone in. It's a prison cell for all intents and purposes and a torture chamber when we need it to be. The walls are three feet thick; there are no windows, no escape, and no one to hear the screams. In the center sits a lone figure. His head is dropped forwards against his chest, arms pulled behind his back, wrists and ankles bound to the plastic chair beneath him.

I take the packet of cigarettes from my inside jacket pocket and pluck one out, placing it between my lips and lighting it. Moving slowly towards the prone figure in the middle of the room, I inhale a deep lungful of smoke and hold it.

"Have you enjoyed your stay with us, Gerard?" I smirk, coming to a halt in front of him.

The Port Authority Chief lifts his head, squinting against the bright fluorescent lights. Deep shadows have taken up residence beneath his eyes but other than that his face is unmarked. When dealing with public figures, it's wise not to mark their face. The body...well, that's fair game. He sways backwards and forwards in his seat but says nothing. "You fucked me over, Gerard." I hand in my pocket.

He shakes his head weakly. "I didn't."

"Don't fucking lie to me!" I flick the cigarette towards his feet. "I know you had my shipment seized. I know you spoke to O'Hara and tipped him off. You're not in my good graces, Mr Brown."

"I had no choice!" he wails, voice cracking.

Tilting my head to the side, I release a long breath. "There's always a choice. Now, I'm going to give you the opportunity to make the right one."

"I can't help you," he says, gritting his teeth. "You can't just kidnap me. Someone will notice I'm gone. I have a wife. She'll report me missing," he says desperately, and I smile.

"Like I said, we all have a choice." I take my phone from my pocket and dial Una's number, putting the call on loudspeaker. The ring tone echoes off the concrete walls, resonating around the room.

The line clicks and the sound of a woman sobbing fills the room. "Gerard?" Her breath hitches.

"Hannah!" he shouts, but the sound of her cries cut off.

"Hello, Gerard," Una purrs. "You remember me, don't you?" I can hear the amusement in her voice as she toys with him like a cat with a mouse.

Gerard's terrified gaze meets mine, and I cock a brow. "She's the hot psycho blonde who threatened to take your eye out, in case you forgot. Time to make a choice, Gerard. I want control over all of the docks that Finnegan O'Hara has." I turn my back on him, pacing a few steps away. "And you want your wife safe. I get what I want, and you get what you want. Everyone's a winner."

A bead of sweat rolls over his forehead. "Please don't hurt her."

"Una isn't known for her patience, are you, Morte?"

"I'm feeling generous. I'll count to three." The whimpering in the background escalates to desperate screams.

"One. Two —"

"No!" Gerard cries. "Please, please. I'll do it."

I smile. "That's a good choice Mr. Brown, and I'll remind you now that if you betray me, if you let me down, don't think that I won't go to little Gracie's school or pay your wife another visit."

He drops his head forward and sniffs pathetically. "Please don't hurt them."

"That's all on you, Gerard. I want everything O'Hara had before his unfortunate demise." I pat his shoulder.

"He...he's dead?"

"Guess I forgot to mention that. I thought you needed the proper encouragement to remain loyal. After all, loyalties are so frivolous nowadays." I turn to Gio. "Cut him loose and have him taken back to his wife." I leave the room, placing the phone to my ear. "Okay, you can leave now," I tell Una.

"I was hoping that would be more exciting."

"You can try and make me bleed later if you're feeling that violent."

"Remember you said that." She hangs up and my dick's hard just at the thought of it. The woman has me by the balls.

"Nero." I turn around halfway up the stairs. Gio is standing in the doorway and pulls the heavy metal door closed behind him. "Andre came through." Andre Paro is the guy to know in Mexico, he's somewhat of a broker, liaising between cartels and cutting deals that no one wants to make in person. "I wired a hundred grand to him this morning. He's overseeing the girl's transfer to Rafael as we speak." Rafael D'Cruze is at the top of the Juarez Cartel, and my supplier. I don't fully trust him, but the likelihood of the Sinaloa selling Anna to me is slim. The fact that an Italian is interested in an unknown Mexican sex slave would raise suspicion, whereas Rafael has more weight and respect in South America. If the sale comes from him, they almost can't reject it. Of course, originally, I planned for her to stay with him until Una completed the job, almost like a pay half now half later deal, but well, this is no longer a simple exchange of favors. The lines are blurred, and motivations are called into question. I don't believe for a second that Una would still be here without the leverage of her sister, and I have no intention of giving her Anna just yet, but as each day passes, the plan I had set out seems less and less important. In order to get to the end game though I have to let it play out. I have to let the chips fall and give Una the chance to do the very thing I sought her out for. The plan is what matters, all that can matter, which means Una is still the queen, and valuable as she is, she's still only a piece on the board.

22

UNA

I t's been a week since Nero killed O'Hara and now here we are, ready to take out the rest of his list. He called a truce and of course they agreed to it, because they're mafia and they believe there's honor among thieves, but they don't know Nero, or they just aren't paying attention, because I had him pegged in one look. For Nero, boundaries don't exist and ethics are laughable. I think that's what makes me want him. I haven't felt truly safe in a very long time, but Nero manages to make me feel protected in a world where I'm the predator, because sometimes, in order to fight the monsters under the bed, you need a monster of your own.

Nero stands in the doorway of the dining room, his arms folded over his chest as he watches me strip down my rifle. My baby, my pride and joy. Actually, that's a lie, because I have twelve exact replicas of the same gun stored in various places around the globe. It's a custom .25 calibre assault rifle. I clean and oil the pieces, going through it methodically, like a ritual. I need this; the calm before the storm. This…being here with Nero; it's throwing me off.

Now more than ever I need to cling to my cool indifference, the training that's so ingrained.

I don't look up at Nero, but I hear him move closer. "Nice gun."

I spare him a brief glance. "Thanks." He's wearing a black suit with a white shirt. The jacket is draped casually over his shoulder. His hair is tidier than usual and the confidence he wears so easily looks strained, even masked behind the intimidating stance that he can't turn off. If I'm a chameleon then Nero is a big cat, roaring and baring his teeth, unapologetic about exactly what he is. The irony is, he doesn't even need the teeth. His power is growing, even in the short time I've been here. Sasha has his ear to the ground for me. I've told him I'm working a job for the Italians. Nothing else. But he keeps me informed, tells me about the whisperings of the New York capo so ruthless the rest of the mafia fear him. Marco Fiore has been heard to call Nero a rabid dog, and talk like that will get him killed.

"Nervous?" I smirk.

He tilts his head and whatever lack of confidence I saw a second ago disappears. He circles around behind me, and I fight the urge to turn and keep him in my eye line. I steel my spine and focus on taking a bullet from the ammo box, placing it on the table in front of me. A tremor works over my skin, an awareness of the dangerous presence so close, lingering right behind me. I may fuck him, and to a certain degree trust him, but not completely. Dealing with Nero is like walking on a knife's edge, feeling the cold bite of the blade on the soles of my feet and finding a sick satisfaction in it. He's a dangerous and twisted adrenaline rush, not unlike the same thrill I get when I kill. His fingers brush my neck and my breath hitches as he scoops my hair up in one hand. He yanks my head to the side so hard my scalp burns, but the pain is lost as hot breath blows over my skin, followed by the scrape of his teeth. "Don't miss."

I click a bullet into the chamber. "I never miss."

"Good." He steps away.

Calm. Focus. The icy anticipation of the kill. That's what I need. The images running through my mind at this second are anything but...

23

NERO

Marco is already here when I arrive. He sits at the table, a smoking cigar in the ashtray in front of him. He's in his mid-forties, his dark hair is streaked with grey. Marco is one of those guys in the mafia without an official role, yet influential. He's involved in our legitimate businesses, has the ear of Arnaldo…that kind of shit. The mob consists of Made men, soldiers, and the capo controls the soldiers. There are two New York capos and I'm one of them. I manage the family's interests, ensure that the people who pay us are protected, manage the influx of drugs and weapons in and out of my area of the city. Or at least that's what most people think. The men I've invited to this meeting, the men I want dead, they're the ones who see me for what I really am. I'm someone who can't be put in a box and neatly labelled. What I want goes beyond that. I want power. Absolute power. I will kill whomever I need to, buy the ones I can't and destroy anyone and anything who gets in my way. They see it and it rattles them. As it should. They supported Lorenzo because he was an idiot and idiots are easily controlled.

The key to control is to ensure that the people in charge, the people with the supposed power never really have any. Lorenzo may have been the capo, but politics are politics, and even the president has to answer to those beneath him. I don't. I won't, and they see it. It almost seems a shame to kill the few astute men in my organization, but if they're not allies then they're enemies and a wise enemy makes for an ominous one.

"Nero." Marco stands, holding his arms out to the side to embrace me, but it's also an invitation to check him for weapons. I embrace him and he kisses both my cheeks, smiling wide like I'm his best friend. I keep it brief, eyeing the two men he brought with him. He's not carrying but I can guarantee they are. Gio shifts behind me, and I can tell he's thinking the same thing. I brought him instead of Jackson because he's intelligent and calculated. Not rash.

A few seconds later, Bernardo Caro and Franco Lama walk in. Bernardo is the other New York capo and Franco is his savage right-hand with way too much power for my liking. Bernardo embraces me as Marco did, but Franco lingers behind. The three of us take a seat at the table.

"It is a shame you have not invited us to talk sooner," Marco says in our native language. This is at the heart of his issue, the fact that as the new capo I didn't conform to the bullshit customs of paying respect to this fucker. I did it deliberately. If I wanted to make new friends, I'd throw a tea party. I'm much more partial to a bloodbath. Of course, to win any game, you need someone to play against. Marco, Bernardo and Franco are merely opposing pawns. Their presence is necessary in order for me to cross the board and take the king. And take him, I will.

I'M STARING straight at Marco when the glass window behind him smashes. Two quick fire shots. His eyes go wide, and he falls face down on the table. I barely have a second to catch up before Bernardo goes down, too. Shots are fired inside the room, and bodies hit the floor simultaneously. And then, silence. Gio stands with his gun raised, having killed Marco's guards. A low gurgled groan sounds from the other side of the table, and I approach Franco where he lies on the floor, clutching a bullet wound in his abdomen.

HE GLARES UP AT ME, blood leaking from the corner of his mouth. "You have no honor," he hisses.

I SMILE. "Honor is for people who have a line. I don't." I lift my gun and fire one shot at his head. It's done.

24

UNA

S taring down my scope at Nero, I focus on the way his lips press together. He appears the image of sophistication and calm, but I can see the subtle flutter of the muscle in his jaw. He's pissed off. Well, I guess I had best get this show on the road before he loses his shit and tries to take all my fun.

Focusing on the back of Marco Fiore's head, I take a steadying breath in then out and squeeze the trigger once to crack the window and again to take him out. The double bang explodes around the alleyway between this building and the one I'm firing on. I've marked every target in the room, but I have to be quick. Bernardo dives for the ground but I catch him in the side of the head. Franco is almost out of sight. I panic and hurry the shot, hitting him in the gut. Fuck. I don't like messy kills, and I certainly don't like to leave any possibility that they might survive. He's out of sight now, so if he's still alive, Nero or Gio are going to have to finish him off. Pausing for a minute, I wait. Nero pops up, because of course, he knows who the shooter is. He's safe. I allow him to approach

Franco's body and he says something before pointing a gun at him and pulling the trigger. He stares out the window, and even though I know he can't see me, when I stare down the scope he's staring right at me. I line the shot up and smile as I pull the trigger, hitting him in the shoulder. The impact makes his body jerk before he goes down. What can I say? Something to remember me by when I'm gone.

Smiling, I push up off my stomach, disassembling the gun quickly and putting the pieces back in the case. And my last gift for Nero...plausible deniability. I take the card from my pocket - the queen of aces – and press my lips to the back of the card, leaving a bright red lipstick mark. I throw it on the ground amongst the four spent shell casings. The Italians will come looking, and this is what they'll find. It will either halt their search right there, or put a price on my head.

Exiting the abandoned apartment, I pull my hood low over my eyes as I make my way down the fire escape. My black Mercedes lays cloaked in shadow in the alley at the back of the building and I jog to it. I jump in the car and pull away from the scene of the crime. That's it, I'm done. I took out Nero's guys; I fulfilled my end of the bargain. I'll stay here long enough to make sure he follows through with his end and then... then I'm gone. Anna and I will go somewhere no one can find us.

Freedom has always seemed like such a sweet and alluring prospect and yet now that I'm faced with it, I'm not sure what it really means. Nero is, in a way, a captor, a villain bribing and coercing me to do his bidding, and yet, somewhere along the way he became a dark savior I didn't even know I needed. He makes me feel safe, and in my world, safety is like a rare and coveted gem. For the first time in my life, I'm torn between what I want to do and what I should do, because I've never *wanted* anything.

When I get back to the apartment, Nero isn't yet back. I jump in the shower, throwing on one of his shirts after I've dried off. I've become unnecessarily fond of wearing them.

I'm in his bedroom, sitting on the edge of the bed when I hear the elevator open. The sewing kit is in here, and if he's already been stitched then he'll be so out of it on painkillers he'll have to sleep it off. Gio helps him into the room and glances at me, a calculating look crossing his features.

"You going to shoot him again?" He eyes the pistol strapped to my thigh, and I smile. Nero scowls at me, but it's lost on a wince as he leans against the wall next to the door.

"Would you believe me if I said it was for your own good?" I bite my bottom lip, trying to suppress a grin as I glance at Nero.

"You can go, Gio." The calm in his voice is both terrifying and exciting.

"Nero, you're bleeding."

"Go!" he says with more bite this time.

Gio sighs and throws a hard look my way. "If you kill him, I will hunt you down."

"If I wanted him dead, he'd be dead. The hunt would be fun though." I blow him a kiss and he scowls before walking out of the room. "He is way too serious."

Nero stalks towards me. My heart pounds until it's all I can hear, the beautiful crescendo rising like a wave. He's a walking promise of pain and retribution right now. The white of his shirt is stained crimson, matching the fury painted on his face.

He shrugs out of his jacket and leans over me, forcing

me to lean back. His face lingers just inches from mine as he strokes his knuckles over my cheek far too gently. Releasing a trembling breath, I'm poised, waiting. Thump-thump, thump-thump, thump-thump. My heart pounds like the drumbeat in a marching band. His fingers leave a sticky damp trail of blood on my cheek before he drags his thumb over my bottom lip. I can practically taste his blood on my tongue as he touches his forehead to mine and closes his eyes. My entire body coils tight like a spring ready to explode, and every single muscle aches with the tension. Lips brush over mine in the whisper of a kiss and I inhale the familiar spicy scent of him, laced with the metallic twang of his blood. When his tongue caresses mine, I moan. It's a distraction from the fingers inching around me throat, squeezing hard enough to cut off my air. I smile.

"You fucking shot me," he growls.

My smile widens, and his eyes flash dangerously. "Plausible deniability," I recite his own words back at him.

"I should just kill you." A cruel smile twists his lips and I gasp when his fingers tighten, pulling me up to meet him.

"You can't kill your queen."

"I no longer need my queen."

"What will it be then, Nero? Kill me or kiss me?"

"Ah, Morte. Both, always both." He shoves me down on the mattress and his arm locks, his full weight pressing down on my windpipe, completely cutting off my oxygen. He stares down at me with fire in his eyes. And there it is, his fury –pure, unbridled rage. The monster is out of his cage and he's come to play. This is our natural state. Him, with his hand at my throat, me, fighting him every step of the way, only to succumb eventually.

I claw at his wrist, gasping for air through my closed throat. He presses even harder and my heartbeat pounds so fast, the fear consuming me, driving the adrenaline through my veins. I want it, I always want it. Reaching for him, I grip his shoulder and push my thumb against the bloody patch on his shirt, trying to feel the torn and damaged tissue through the dressing that Gio has haphazardly applied. He roars and rears back. Seizing the opportunity, I maneuver him onto his back.

"Play nice," I say, straddling his body and leaning over him. Using the heel of my hand, I press against his shoulder, making him hiss out a breath. With very little warning, he explodes upright, catching me by surprise and shredding the material of his own shirt from my body in a fit of rage. I love that in the heat of the moment he's an unpredictable creature, ruled by his violent nature. His bullet wound doesn't seem to bother him as I wrench the buttons of his shirt open. His lips move over my neck angrily, kissing, biting, sucking down the column of my throat and over my collarbone. He tosses me on the bed and flips me onto my front as if I weigh nothing. I hear the clink of his belt buckle, the rustle of material... My body trembles with anticipation, my skin flushing in goose bumps as I wait for the heat of his touch. Fingers dig into my hips, dragging me across the mattress before he lifts my hips. The hot skin of his chest meets my back as I push up on my hands and knees, his body folding over mine. The steady drops of blood hit my shoulder blade before rolling down my side and dropping on the bed. The red spots mar the pale grey of the sheets beneath it, crimson spreading and staining the fibers. Blood and sex are such a heady combination, the evidence of violence only feeding the desire I have for him. His hand meets the back of my neck and he forces my face down onto the bed. I get no warning before his fingers are pushing inside my pussy, making me bite down on my own arm to stifle a moan.

"So fucking wet. Shooting me does it for you, hey?" He pulls out and pushes back in again.

"I like you angry."

"Oh, baby, I'm fucking angry all right." His fingers leave me, and I barely have time to register any movement before his dick slams inside me so hard I'm winded. A strangled sound escapes my throat as I choke on a pained groan. He doesn't give me a chance to recover before he's pounding into me like he hates me. I smile, relishing in every single inch of his rage. "I'm going to tear you in two before I'm fucking done." And he very nearly does. The entire time I can feel the steady dripping of his blood on my back. I let out a feral growl as he hits a point so deep it feels like he's trying to crawl inside me.

"Yes. Break me, Nero," I beg, hoping for his brand of destruction, seeking a punishment and a salvation that only his unbridled rage can mete out. He drives into me even harder and the pain blends with a deep-seated plea-sure, pushing me to a place I've never felt before. My core clenches hard and everything explodes outwards, sending waves of pleasure shooting through every single muscle in my body. His name falls from my lips over and over like a curse, and he stiffens behind me on a roar. When he pulls away, he instantly collapses on the bed. I lie there, desperately trying to catch my breath. That was…uncontrolled. I've spent my whole life chasing control, and distance, and striving to be rational at all times, and suddenly, he has me craving the opposite of all those things.

I like walking that fine line, fucking him while knowing we could very well kill each other the second it's over. Needing each other, wanting each other, knowing that we're the last thing either of us should be running towards, or maybe I'm wrong. Maybe we're exactly what each other needs. I embrace Nero, my depraved reflection staring right back at me.

I turn my head to the side, glancing at him. His chest rises and falls in deep swells and a thin sheen of sweat covers his skin. Blood is steadily seeping through the dressing at his shoulder. "You're bleeding," I whisper, brushing my fingers over the sticky, wet dressing.

His fingers wrap around my wrist, the grip bruising. "It's fine. The doctor will be here soon."

I sit up, slowly peeling the dressing away from his skin. The neat bullet hole pumps blood steadily. Normally, it wouldn't be an issue, but it's been an hour since I shot him and now his heart rate is elevated. "I'll be back." I get up and take one of his shirts from his closet. Downstairs, I open my rifle case, plucking a single round from its spot nestled in the foam interior. I then grab the cleaning rod that I left in the dining room earlier.

When I get back to the bedroom, Nero hasn't moved. He lies there with his eyes closed, a red stain spreading across the duvet beneath him.

"I need you to sit up. This is going to hurt." His eyes open and he snorts as he follows my instruction.

"More than being shot?"

"A lot more." He glares at me, and I shrug. "Do you want to bleed out?"

He blinks and it takes him a long second before his eyes open again. Placing the tip of the bullet between my teeth, I pop the head off the casing. The wound is a through and through, and the only way to heal it quickly... well, it's not pleasant but it's worth it. I pull the dressing off his back and place the back of the casing against the bullet wound. Glancing at his face quickly, I take a deep breath and shove it inside. His eyes go wide, and he grits his teeth, snarling.

"What the fuck are you doing?"

"Stop being a baby." I press the cleaning rod into the open end of the casing and push, forcing the casing through the open wound. He growls and I'm pretty sure he's going to hit me before I can get it all the way through. The bullet pops out the front of his shoulder and the bleeding quickens. Nero is swaying dangerously, his breaths becoming fast and hard.

Blood steadily runs down his body, flowing over his muscular stomach until it soaks into the seam of his boxers. Grabbing his jacket off the floor, I take his lighter from the pocket, flipping the top back. He frowns and eyes it through drooped eyelids. "What are you doing with that?" His words are slurring slightly now from blood loss and pain.

"I'm sorry." I've had this done to me and it's the worst pain I've ever experienced. Coming from me, that's saying a lot. I move the flame closer to him, holding it to the edge of the wound. A small spark catches and he roars like a wounded beast. Every single muscle in his body contracts and a vein at his temple throbs erratically before he collapses back against the pillows. He drifts on the verge of consciousness, his chest rising and falling rapidly. By pushing the bullet casing through the wound, it leaves a trail of gunpowder. Light it and it instantly cauterizes the wound, killing any infection and stopping the bleeding. It will heal the wound a lot faster, but it hurts worse than the original bullet.

Picking up his legs, I move them, positioning him on the bed. I take the small syringe of morphine that I left beside the sewing kit earlier and slide it into the vein on the inside of his forearm. Within seconds his eyes close and he's out for the count. Maneuvering his unconscious body enough to put dressings on both the entrance and exit wound is not easy feat. He weighs a ton. I hesitate at the edge of the bed, before telling myself I should sleep with him, to keep an eye on him. The steady rhythm of his breathing lulls me to sleep.

The scene unfolds before me, exactly as it has so many times before. Nicholai stands beside me and thrusts the gun into my shaking hand. The tightness wraps itself around my chest, and the guilt and grief rush up around me until I'm drowning in their murky depths. I look at the far wall, to where Alex is chained; only this time, it's not Alex. Nero stares back at me, his face perfect and unmarked, his hard, muscular torso bare and without a trace of the blood that usually features in this dream.

Nicholai brushes that tendril of hair away from my face. "Become what you were meant to be, little dove." His thumb trails over my jaw, and I close my eyes as a tear slips down my cheek. "Put a bullet in his head or put a bullet in your own," he grates, his lips brushing the side of my face.

I open my eyes and instead of seeing Alex begging me to shoot him, Nero demands that I do so. A small smile pulls at his lips and my arm moves of its own volition, lifting the gun as if I were nothing more than a puppet on a string. Panic starts to bubble up my throat and my breathing becomes frantic as I try desperately to lower the gun. I stare at Nero, tears tracking down my face as I realize what is about to happen.

He stares back at me, a cocky smile plastered on his lips. "Do your worst, Morte."

My finger twitches over the trigger and the bang echoes around the room before his body slumps forward against the restraints.

"Nero!" I scream and fall to my knees.

Jolting awake, I gasp, I can't breathe. My vision is blurred with tears and my entire body is shaking as I struggle for air. Nero lets out a pained grunt and then his hand lands on my face before he falls back against the pillows, breath hissing through his teeth. I swipe angrily at the treacherous tears as I slide out of the bed. All I can hear is Nicholai's voice in my head; *You are a weapon and weapons don't weep.*

"Where are you going, Morte?" Every word he says is strained, and I know how much pain he must be in.

"I'll be back." I take the opportunity to go to the kitchen, grabbing the medical kit. There are various painkillers in there and a couple more bottles of morphine. Grabbing a syringe and needle, I head back to the room. The memory of the dream replays in my head like a bad horror film, and I'm shaken, not by the notion of having the dream, but of the fact that shooting him upset me so much. I can't remember ever feeling such a sense of loss, not even when I killed Alex. I loved Alex, but in a way I always knew it would end badly. We grew up in hell and he was never strong enough to bear the atrocities there. He was too good, too kind, loved too hard and sacrificed too much. Nero, on the other hand, always seems so indestructible to me, so utterly implacable, like a cliff face standing against a hurricane. Nero isn't Alex, Nero is more. And didn't I always know that I was a danger to him, just as he was a danger to me? The dream hit too close, felt too real.

Returning to the bedroom, I sit on the edge of the bed, turning the bedside lamp on. Nero squints against the light as he turns his face towards me. He looks pale, the usual golden tan absent from his skin. He stares at me and I drop my eyes to the bottles in my hand, focusing on opening the syringe packet.

He grips my chin with strong fingers and forces me to look at him. "Don't hide from me, Morte."

"I'm not."

His thumb swipes over the corner of my eye. "You're fucking beautiful when you cry." I squeeze my eyes shut and his thumb trails over my cheek. "Tell me about your dream. You screamed my name. Did I hurt you?" I open my eyes and focus on his lips, because I don't want to look in his eyes. "Tell me what could possibly make *death* cry," he whispers, withdrawing his touch.

"I shot you," I admit.

"Yes, you did," he says dryly, those dark eyes watching me closely.

I shake my head. "I killed you."

"You've killed a lot of people."

"This…" My voice gets stuck in my throat. "This was different. I felt like …like a monster," I rasp. I can't tell him that the reason I felt so horrible is because pulling the trigger damn near tore me apart. I don't want to care for him.

"Because you are. Embrace the monster inside you or become consumed by it. That is the difference between brilliance and insanity, Morte."

He crooks a finger at me. Wordlessly, I climb onto his lap, straddling his thighs. My lips press over his and all the noise in my head goes silent, because nothing outside of him exists for these few seconds. This connection I have to him makes me feel safe, he makes me feel safe, and that scares the shit out of me because people like us, we're never safe. He's dark and twisted but so am I, and I want to bask in his depravity. I want to be held by him and feel protected in the knowledge that he is that which others fear. Pressing my forehead to his, I close my eyes, breathing him in. We both know that whatever this is, it's temporary, but for now, I want to experience something I've never had. Him. This. Us.

———

WHEN I WAKE up in the morning, Nero is still out of it. I dosed him up on morphine before we fell asleep last night and his chest rises and falls evenly with heavy breaths. His arm is wrapped around my waist, pulling me tightly into his side. I brush my fingers over the warm, smooth skin of his chest, wanting to stay this close to his blistering heat, because he makes me feel as though I'll never be cold again.

I jump when my phone rings, buzzing against the bedside table like a pneumatic drill. Hurrying to disentangle myself from Nero's hold, I quickly pick it up, glancing at the screen. Shit. Getting out of the bed, I leave the room, quietly closing the door behind me before I answer.

"Nicholai."

"Ah, little dove." He croons in Russian. "I have missed you."

"I've missed you, too." It's more a false of habit than anything, but I do have an affection for Nicholai, a bond of sorts, in as much capacity as I have.

"I have a job for you. Very important, a personal favor for a friend. He requested you." A thousand thoughts rush through my mind, but the main one is that I'll have to leave, but of course, I will. I was always going to have to.

"Where?"

"Miami. Your flight is already booked from JFK this afternoon." Shit, that's fast. "It is an urgent job. You have a forty-eight hour deadline and then your target will leave the country."

"Okay. Do you have an in for me?" Most jobs, I have to do my own reconnaissance, but with only two days, the client usually lays out some form of set up and Sasha does the rest.

"I have Sasha here for you." There's a moment of silence before Sasha's voice comes over the line.

"Your target is Diego Rosso," he says. Diego Rosso is a

Cuban weapons dealer with a nasty habit of selling weapons to pretty much anyone who wants to buy them. He's actually number eighteen on the FBI's most wanted list, due to his rather friendly relationship with terrorists in Syria and Iraq. His name has popped up several times over the last few years, and I'm familiar with his network.

"I've looked at his credit card statements and it seems that whenever he's in Miami he sends multiple transactions to an escort agency." He's all business. "I hacked the agency's server and they have a booking tomorrow for one Mr. Julian Torres, an alias of his."

"The girl he booked?"

"I'm sending you her name and address now."

"Thanks." I hang up and linger in the hallway, bracing my back against the wall and pressing the top of the phone against my chin as I think through everything I need to do to tie up here. There is no amount of tying that can make leaving okay though, because, for once in my life, the next kill has lost its appeal. My main concern is Anna. I've done Nero's job, now he needs to do his. I'll do this hit, but I will be back, and I will keep coming back for as long as it takes him to find her. Going downstairs, I pack up my shit. Guns, ammo, cash, the laptop. I can't take it with me, but I'll put it back in the storage locker. I then go upstairs, taking each step slowly before I walk down the hallway. My hand hovers over the handle of his bedroom door, and I almost don't want to go in. I could just leave a note and go, but that would be weak, and I don't do weak.

25

NERO

"Nero?" I wake at the sound of Una's voice. She's fully dressed in her black combat pants and long-sleeved shirt. Her hair is loose around her shoulders, and a troubled expression mars her face.

"What's wrong?"

"I held up my end of our deal. I want my sister," she says coldly.

I stare at her for a second, trying to see through her defensive bullshit. "And you'll have her. She's in Juarez with one of my contacts."

Her eyes widen. "You've had her this entire time?"

"Since last week. It will take a few days to get her out of Mexico." I push up off the mattress, fighting the urge to just fucking lie back down as the pain tears through the left-hand side of my body. She stands and takes a step back, crossing her arms over her chest. Keeping my left arm clutched to my body, I climb to my feet and head towards the bathroom, ignoring Una. Every step feels like someone is punching me in the shoulder and Una really isn't my favorite person right now.

"I'll be back in a few days," she says casually. I freeze halfway across the room and slowly pivot. She clocks the look on my face as I approach and raises her chin, setting her jaw defiantly.

"Back from where?"

"Miami. Nicholai called me in for a job."

Fucking Nicholai. "So, the master has clicked his fingers and off you run?"

Her fists clench before she takes a deep breath. Her loyalty to him is unflinching because she knows no better. Nicholai *is* all she knows. "I'm a hired killer, so yes, when someone needs killing, I go."

We stare at each other for a long moment, because I want to stop her and she knows it, but I won't, and we both know that too. "Then go."

"Be careful," she whispers, jerking her chin towards my shoulder.

"Shouldn't I be saying that to you?"

A wry smile pulls at her lips. "I'm the kiss of death."

Unable to keep distance between us, I step forward and wrap my free hand around the back of her neck, yanking her close. "No, Morte, you're mine." My lips brush her cheek. "Remember that." I nip her jaw then step back. Words that neither of us are prepared to speak swirl between us, thickening the air with tension. I turn away and go into the bathroom.

Closing the door, I brace my back against it and wait for her to leave. The second I hear her retreating footsteps fade, I pick up the nearest thing, a bottle of hand wash, and launch it at the mirror. The glass smashes, splintering and throwing my own broken reflection back at me. Pain flashes through my shoulder. She's both literally and metaphorically burned me from the inside out, because I want her to the point of irrationality. A possessive rage clings to the edges of my mind.

I know how Una gets to her clients and the imagine of her kissing another guy, allowing him to touch her, wanting him to bury his face in her neck so that she can render him weak and thrust a knife in his back... I see it all so clearly and it's driving me fucking insane. Una is mine, and she can't outrun that.

———

UNA'S BEEN GONE for a total of six hours, and as much as I try to work, try not to think about her, I can't. The idea of her on a job plagues me, aggravating me. I know when she seduces a client it's not real, but they don't, they think they have a right to her for a few minutes, and even though she kills them for their troubles, it's not enough.

My phone rings, tearing me from my thoughts. The screen flashes showing a south American number. I pick it up.

"Yeah."

"Nero, I have some information that might interest you." Rafael. His Spanish accent is slight but distinctive.

"And what is this information going to cost me?"

"Consider it a favor to a friend." We're definitely not friends. Business acquaintances but not friends. "I hear that you are acquainted with the mad Russians favorite pet." The irony that he's keeping said pets own sister and he doesn't even know it...

"What about her?"

He pauses and draws a long breath. "I have heard she's very pretty, much like her sister. It would be a shame for her to meet her end." How the fuck does he know that Anna is Una's sister? No one knows that she even has a sister apart from me, her and Anna, but of course he has Anna. There's no telling what information the bastard would try and pry from her. I say nothing because in this situation words are dangerous. He huffs another laugh. "Five million dollars is a lot of money."

"Five million dollars for what?" I snap.

"The price on her pretty little head of course. I hear the Los Zetas sent their best sicario for her. He's in Miami now. I wonder if the angel of death is as good as they say."

"This favor of yours, is there a price tag on it?"

"Just remember it." In other words, he'll call it in at some point. "Tick tock, Nero. Run capo, run capo, run, run, run." He sings before laughing and hanging up.

26

UNA

I normally love Miami, but I think I'm coming down with something and the heat and humidity aren't helping the nausea that's settled into the pit of my stomach since I left Nero yesterday. The car rolls to a stop on a quiet street beneath the shade of a palm tree and I step out.

Elaina Matthews' apartment is in a small building near South beach. It's non-descript, with a set of iron stairs and a walkway that runs along the first floor. Knocking on her door, I wait, hearing the shuffle of footsteps on the other side.

She opens the door in a tracksuit, a pile of blonde hair scooped up on top of her head.

"Yeah?" Her eyebrows pinch together in a frown.

I could probably think of a hundred reasons to have her invite me in, but my head is pounding, and I can't be bothered with the niceties. Instead, I ram my shoulder into her, pushing her back into the apartment.

"Hey!" Slamming the door behind me, I thrust the

needle of the small syringe into her neck, depressing the plunger. She reaches for her neck before her eyelids start to droop. The mixture of Ketamine and Rohypnol works quickly and will knock her out for at least eight hours. When she wakes up, she won't remember a thing.

That takes her out of the equation.

———

TUGGING at the hem of my tiny dress, I take the short walk down Ocean Drive to the Beacon Hotel. The street is packed, and it feels like a carnival. There are people everywhere, street performers, girls in bikinis walking up and down holding up signs for various bars. The sidewalk is littered with tables and chairs as the bars sprawl out into the street. People sit drinking cocktails from glasses the size of my head, the liquid smoking and bubbling like a witch's cauldron. Cars crawl along the beach front, chromed out Cadillacs and supped-up sports cars revving their engines and blasting hip-hop music. It's like a street party, and actually, I don't look even slightly out of place in my slutty dress. The number of people coupled with all the music blasting out of each bar has my senses in overload. I can't help but want to listen and probe the area around me for possible threats. I swear I can feel eyes on me, but I can't sense anything past all the noise. Glancing over my shoulder, I attempt to check for followers. The crowd is so dense, I couldn't tell you even if an attacker were right behind me.

I quicken my pace until I reach the hotel. It's an art deco building, slap bang in the middle of the bars and clubs, and honestly, if I were a wanted weapons dealer, it's a location I would pick. If he needs to escape quickly, he could disappear into the swelling crowd in seconds, slip into any one of ten bars that I can see from here. It's a smart move, but I'm not the FBI, I'm not here to cuff him. He won't be running from me.

Stepping inside, I inhale a breath of the cool, conditioned air. Tiled flooring clicks beneath my heels and I glance up to the curved viewing gallery above. A bar opens up to my right, and I instantly spot Diego. The picture Sasha sent me was a blurred surveillance image, but it's enough. Approaching him, I hop up on the stool beside him and order a vodka without sparing him a glance. The barman moves away to make my drink and I twist my face towards him.

He has that typical Miami look with the linen pants and a white shirt, top three buttons undone. Black chest hair peeks through the gap in his shirt and a heavy gold chain hangs around his neck. His hair is shaved almost to his head. He's just an average-looking guy, I suppose.

"Julian?"

He glances in my direction, holding his glass in one hand and a cigarette in the other. As soon as I inhale the smell, it reminds me of Nero, the scent of smoke and expensive cologne. Diego brings the cigarette to his lips, smiling around the filter tip and making it seem like the dirty habit it really is. Whereas Nero can make the simple act of smoking a cigarette look like a work of art.

"Who are you?" His accent is a strange mix of American, Cuban and Spanish.

"My name is Isabelle. The agency sent me." I hold my hand out to him and flash him a blinding smile.

"Where is Elaina?" he asks, suspicion lacing his voice. Shit.

"She couldn't make it. The agency thought you might

like me instead." I push as much seduction into my voice as possible and his expression softens.

Eyes skate over my body, locking onto the point where the miniscule dress clings to my upper thighs. Lifting his drink towards his lips, he nods. Jesus, how to make a girl feel good about herself. The barman places my drink on the bar and I take a large gulp of the shit vodka.

"Are you from Miami?" I ask.

He downs his drink and slams the glass on the bar a little too hard. "I didn't come here to talk to you."

I smirk because I'm going to enjoy killing this one. "Of course." I neck the remainder of the vodka. "Shall we?"

Standing up, he surprises me by offering his hand. I take it, my fingers brushing over the thick callouses of his palm, which is good, because then he won't notice how equally calloused my hands are. I can pull on a mask and become anyone I need to be, but once a fighter always a fighter and the evidence simply can't be hidden. My knuckles are thick with scar tissue, the silvery white skin marked from splitting open and healing time and time again. It's given me away once or twice.

I allow him to glide his hand around my waist, fighting my less civilized instincts as he leads me out of the bar. Soon, I tell the angry little demon inside my head. The second he gets me in the elevator, I'm pressed against the mirrored wall with his lips on my neck and his hands on my exposed thighs. The doors open, he drags me out, and I play along, allowing him to force me backwards along the corridor. Jeez, when was the last time the guy got laid? My back hits a door and his hand is practically in my underwear as he fumbles with the key card. This usually wouldn't bother me, my cold detachment allowing me to see it as just part of the job. But today I have to grit my teeth and bite back the bile that's rising in my throat. Just a few more seconds. His lips slam over mine and he shoves me into the room.

The door clicks shut, and the second I'm thrown into darkness, a fissure of unease crawls through me. Something's wrong. "You make a shit whore." No sooner have the words sunk in than his hand slams around my throat, almost taking me off my feet as he throws me into a bedside table. I groan, blinking as my eyes adjust to the faint light drifting through the window. A lamp has fallen to the floor beside me and I reach for it, unclicking the light bulb as he closes in on me again. I get to my feet just in time to ram the bulb into his face. It smashes, embedding jagged shards into his skin. He shouts out something in Spanish as the blood pours down his cheek. I nail him in the kidney and he hits me in the face so hard, I almost go down again. Jesus, who is this guy?

Spitting out a mouthful of blood, I crack my neck to the side before going for him again. For every blow I dish out, he gives me one twice as hard. The last time I fought like this I was in training. This is a fight to the death and we both know it. Launching me onto the bed, he lands on top of me, hands clamping around my throat. He doesn't bother with a gentle easing in. No, the grip is hard enough to break my neck, never mind choke me. I crack him in the side of the temple, but it does nothing. Pulling my mind together, I force myself to think and not panic. *Embrace death.* My right hand is pressed between our bodies, if I can just…I manage to move my wrist enough to drop the silver blade from my cuff, and then I jab him in the crotch with it twice. He roars and leaps back off me. Precious air filters into my lungs, dragging a cough from me as I roll onto my front. He grabs me by the back of my neck and tosses me across the room before following and pinning me against the wall with his forearm across my throat.

"Va a ser un buen premio, ángel de la muerte," he hisses in my face. *You will make a fine prize, angel of death.* Only the Mexicans call me that. What the hell did I do to piss them off? He pushes his whole weight against my throat and my nails rake over his face. I press my thumbs into his eyes and he snarls...BANG! Pain slices across my forearm and then he drops to the floor, dead. I whirl to face a shadowy figure rising from the chair in the corner of the room.

"You're losing your touch, morte."

Nero. What the hell? I hold up my finger and bend over, bracing my hands on my knees as I try and breathe through my battered larynx. Glancing at my forearm I note the bright red line, a bullet burn. Motherfucker. "I had that. And what the hell are you doing here?"

I straighten as he approaches me, dragging his eyes slowly over my exposed body. "Working are we?" Glaring, I tug at the hem of my dress which has ridden up, exposing my underwear.

"Why. Are. You. Here?"

Like a snake, he strikes, fingers squeezing my chin to the point of pain. Anger swirls in his irises like an impending storm and the muscles in his jaw contract irritably.

"Were you going to fuck him?" His voice is a low growl.

"What?!"

"Were you going to fuck the sicario?" he repeats, his tone measured and quiet, which is always worrying. The tension rolling off him is thick and turbulent, a pre-cursor to something much more violent.

"I was going to kill him. Or did that little show down look romantic to you? In fact, don't answer that." That's Nero's idea of perfect foreplay.

"If he hadn't tried to kill you?" Hot breath washes over my face, and I can't help the frantic rush of my heart as his potent brand of lust and fear caresses my senses.

"I really think you're missing the important point, which is that he tried to fucking kill me!"

He tilts my head back with a violent shove, bringing his lips close to my ear. "Listen very carefully, Morte. You can run, you can put half the world between us if you like, I don't care. But you are mine. That pussy is mine. These lips are fucking mine." He pulls back and swipes his thumb roughly over my bottom lip. "Kiss another man again, and you won't like what happens next." My stomach tightens along with his grip. So, that's why he let me take a beating, because he's butt hurt that the Mexican kissed me. It's a job! I'll never understand jealousy.

"Were you following me?" He doesn't answer and I shake my head. "You're crazy." I dig my nails into his wrist, and his forehead touches mine on a deep breath.

"This was a set-up. Someone wants you dead. He's one of the best sicarios the Los Zetas has to offer."

"Someone always wants me dead, Nero." Although I've never had any run-ins with the Los Zetas. At least I can feel better about nearly having my ass handed to me though. Those guys are badass.

His grip on my jaw softens, fingers stroking over my cheek. "Enough to pay five million for the hit?"

My eyes go wide, and I glance at the body. Five million. Jesus. "How did you know?"

"I have contacts." Every time I think I know the extent of Nero's power, he surprises me. "Nicholai put you on this job?"

My mind starts spinning through the web of potential betrayal. "Nicholai would never betray me."

"You're an asset to him. And an asset that is now

compromised. If he doesn't want you dead then someone else does, and he's selling you upriver." He steps back and drags both hands through his hair. The beat of music from the street below cuts through the silence that lingers as I try and process the possibility of it all.

"No." I shake my head, scraping my teeth over my bleeding bottom lip. He wouldn't, I know he wouldn't. "He cares about me. He treats me like a daughter."

Nero's burning gaze meets mine, barely restrained anger shining through. "Because it suits him. Do not be naïve. You can't trust him."

No, Nicholai is the only one who has ever cared about me besides Alex. Alex...the boy I shot, the boy he made me shoot. I press my balled-up fist to my forehead and squeeze my eyes shut. If I doubt Nicholai then I doubt everything, every single moment that has led me to this exact point in my life.

"He's using you."

I glare at him, feeling cornered and vulnerable. "Like you did, you mean? And why should I trust you?" My world is crumbling around me. What if it's all just a farce, even Nero?

He tilts his head, his expression cool and impassive. "Because you're mine."

That's it, three words that mean nothing and everything.

"You used me, Nero."

"Yes, and you would do exactly the same, Morte." He's right, I remember thinking the same thing that first night when he mentioned Anna's name. The first rule of negotiation, find something your opponent wants and use it. We're both without morals. We're both born of bloodshed and battle. His knuckles stroke over the side of my neck and my pulse picks up. "You and I are the same, and we would both use everything at our disposal to win. So, let them come. We'll destroy them all." A twisted smile pulls at his lips, and for a moment I feel whole, protected, like I could rely on him. Worse; that I want to. I grab a handful of his thick hair, pulling his face to mine. He kisses me like he owns a piece of me, and he does, because I'm his queen and he's my bloodied king.

W e buy a car with cash and hit the road, heading back to New York. Nero's theory is that I'll be safe within his ranks until I can work out who wants me dead, and then...we kill them. That's all we have to go on for now.

Pulling my knees to my chest, I rest my forehead on them. The confines of the car are making me nauseous again. Great. We've only been on the road for two hours.

"You know, you should stay out of this." The pale blue glow of the dashboard casts his face in an eerie light and his lips curl slightly.

"Morte, from the moment I propositioned you, we were tied. If someone is coming after you, it's because of me."

"Which means they'll be coming for you," I finish. He nods. I study his reaction. "You know who it is."

"I have an idea." He glances at me briefly before turning back to the road. "The hit came the day after the shooting. Only an Italian would be annoyed at the death of three other Italians. Arnaldo knows I was shot, but fuck, I'd be suspicious that only Gio and I managed to escape a massacre."

"He helped you with Lorenzo's assassination though..."

"Yes, but he thought I could be controlled."

"And now you're off book and he's suddenly realized that you can't be leashed."

He nods. "You left the calling card. I walked away with a mild injury. If he knows we're working together then as far as he's concerned, I just bit the hand that feeds me, and so did you."

"It doesn't explain why Nicholai called it in though."

He straightens his arms, pressing his back into the seat. "I don't know, but we trust no one until we have more to go on."

"You could still go back. I can run, and he'll have to come after me. He supported you for capo, so to admit that you went against him would make him look weak. He then goes after the kiss of death, and it looks like he's seeking retribution. No one would ever know you were involved."

He huffs a laugh. "Noble, Morte, but haven't you worked it out yet?" He glances at me and cocks a brow. "I live for war."

"What about Anna?" Nero and I may be willing to fight, but I didn't go through all this to save her, just to drag her into a warzone.

"She'll be safe," he says dismissively, and it instantly makes me suspicious. There's not a lot I can do about it right now though. If I don't save myself, there will be no one to save her.

———

I GRIP the edge of the toilet and throw up into it. This has to be a new low in my life, facing the disgusting toilet bowl of a rest stop bathroom.

"Una!" Nero bangs on the door, rattling the metal lock.

"Give me a second."

This is the second day of this, and I feel like death. I don't get ill, but I've been feeling awful since before Miami. We're just outside Washington though, so we should be in New York at some point tonight. I hear voices outside the bathroom, and it sounds like Nero is arguing with someone before it goes quiet.

"Sweetheart, you need some help?" a heavily accented female voice asks.

Great. I unlock the door and smile politely.

"I'm fine. Thank you." Her eyes trace over my face, and I'm aware that I look like shit. She's a middle-aged woman with peroxide blonde hair and far too much makeup on. A name badge at her chest that reads; Wendy-Anne. She smiles kindly, and I see a flash of pity in her eyes before she shoves her way inside and closes the door.

"How far along?" she asks.

I frown at her. "Sorry, what?" She glances down at my stomach and I follow her gaze. What the hell is she looking at?

"How long ya been throwing up, sweetie?"

"Uh, a couple of days." This is one of those situations where I kind of want to head-butt her, but the motion would probably make me throw up again.

She presses her lips together in a thin line and glances over her shoulder. "You stay here. I'll be back in a jiffy. I told that fella of yours to leave you be." She winks and then steps out of the bathroom. I have no idea what she's doing but my stomach turns over again and I dive for the toilet.

When she comes back, I'm sitting on the dirty floor waiting for the next round of vomiting. "Here ya go, lovey." She hands me a box and I take it, frowning as I read the front.

"A pregnancy test?" I raise my eyebrows. "I'm not pregnant. I'm sterile," I tell her flatly, handing the box back to her. I've been sterile since I was fourteen, all of Nicholai's Elite are.

"My sister, Eileen, she had them tubes tied. Then there she is, forty years old and knocked up." She shakes her head, pushing the box back towards me. "Ain't gonna hurt nothin' to rule it out." She turns and walks out of the room.

"I'm not pregnant!" I call to her retreating back, but she ignores me and closes the door. I stare at the box for a moment, terrified of it. It's impossible, so this is fine. A little white stick falls out when I open the box. Growing up with guys hadn't exactly leant me to know about anything like this. Hell, I grew up learning how to kill people. This wasn't something I ever even thought of, let alone knew about.

Two minutes has never felt so long. I leave the stick on the counter and pace the short circuit from the door to the sink, almost jumping out of my skin when the door bangs. "Una, we need to fucking go," Nero calls.

"Give me a minute."

This is stupid. I'm not pregnant. I pick up the stick, and the two red lines sit in that tiny little window. I read over the instructions three times. Two lines means positive.

"Una!" I startle and drop the stick, scrambling to pick it up and put it in the bin before I open the door. I hope my expression isn't giving away what I'm feeling right now, because if it is, Nero will think someone has died.

"Let's go." I walk straight past him and out the door. Wendy-Anne smiles at me from behind the till, and I manage a small smile back. This sinking, plummeting feeling has settled into my gut and it feels like I'm walking to my own funeral. This is impossible.

NERO

P ulling back the curtain an inch, 1 look out over the parking lot of the shitty motel. The likelihood of anyone coming for us here is slim, but I'm still edgy.

Una has a pistol in pieces on the bed, cleaning it. She's been doing it for the last hour, her brows pulled together and her eyes lost and distant. I know it's Arnaldo who's put a hit on her, just as I suspected he would. But when I put this entire plan into motion, I never for a second thought that I would want her so badly. To own Una body and soul. I want to stand beside her and make our enemies bleed. She's no longer a tool; she's the perfect ally, the perfect complement to everything I am. How do you let that go when you know you'll never find it again? Una is my own personal obsession, my weakness and my strength. Together, we're unstoppable.

Crossing the room, I remove the gun barrel she's been cleaning for the last ten minutes from her hand. I place a finger under her chin and force her to look at me. There's a smudge of gun oil on her cheek, smeared over the porcelain skin. Wide indigo eyes meet mine.

"You only clean your guns before you're about to kill someone. Should I be worried?"

She huffs and falls back against the pillows. "It clears my mind." She's wearing one of my shirts again and it pulls up, showing just a flash of her underwear. The sight of her long, bare legs is enough to make my dick hard. Her eyes shift to the dressing at my shoulder. "Come here, let me look at that."

I move closer to the bed and she crawls to me, getting to her knees so she can peel the dressing away. Her fingers are gentle but firm against my skin. The wound still hurts, because that's what happens when someone shoots you and then sets you on fire. I've stopped taking the painkillers because they cloud my mind, and I need complete clarity. "This looks good," she says under her breath.

"No thanks to you."

"It would be much worse if I hadn't used the gun powder."

"It would be much better if you hadn't shot me."

"You know, you're really hung up on that." Her lips quirk into a smile, and I grip the back of her neck, pulling her close. Those indigo eyes drop to my mouth, her lips parting.

"I figure you owe me."

When I kiss her, she tastes of blood and death and everything I want. My free hand slips up her body and beneath her shirt until I'm brushing her breast. Shoving her back on the bed, I crawl between her thighs. Her chest rises and falls erratically, fingers threading through my hair as I kiss over her hip bone and shove the shirt further and further up her body. She's fucking beautiful; toned curves and pale skin, littered with scars, some faded to silver while

others are still a rich purple. Her body is a portrait of a
hard and violent life, and each and every scar only makes
me harder for her.

She yanks at my belt until it comes undone, and then
grabs my throat, digging her fingers in on either side of my
Adam's apple. When I pull away, she shoves me to my back
on the mattress. Then lands on top of me.

"You just love to fucking push me," I growl, grabbing
her around the throat. We always end up right here
because it's where we belong.

"You know I like you angry." I tighten my grip and a
brilliant smile crosses her face. She looks so perfect; innocence and seduction all wrapped up with a fucked up little
bow on the top as if she were made for me. When I palm
her breast, her body bows, sending white-blonde hair
cascading down her back. Those full lips part on a soft
moan, and I press my thumb inside her mouth. The little
noises she makes and the stroke of her warm tongue nearly
make me explode. Sitting up, I bring us face-to-face, wrapping my arms around her until every naked inch of her is
pressed against me. To the rest of the world, she's the
whisper of death on the wind, feared and revered. And yet
here she is, so beautifully vulnerable and trusting in my
arms. She feels like all the parts of me I didn't even know
were missing, the parts I didn't even want.

The lace of her underwear drags over my cock as she
rolls her hips in a move nothing short of pure torture. I
have no patience when it comes to her, so I grab the crotch
of her panties and tear them away. Her fingers dive into
my hair, yanking, demanding. I grip her hips, equally as
demanding as I force her down on my waiting cock. The
trembling of her body is so beautiful. Her pussy feels like
the closest I'll ever get to heaven. She touches her forehead
to mine and I close my eyes, feeling her rapid breaths blow

over my face. We stay like that for a second, her clinging to my shoulders while I imprison her against me. Her hips begin to roll lazily, and I bite back a groan. I've fucked Una a lot but every time feels more intense than the last. She's like a slow burn scorching everything she touches, and fuck, if I don't want her to incinerate me. I trail my hands up her back, feeling the ancient bumps and welts of long worn scars. And when she comes, it's like art and music blended into one perfect masterpiece. I bite her bottom lip, swallowing her moans as her pussy clamps down on me. It's enough to make me explode inside her and collapse back on the mattress.

I turn to face Una where she lays beside me, but her expression is distant, detached. Something's wrong with her, and I'd say it's the threat of death, but as she said herself, someone always wants her dead. It's more than that. She gets up and goes into the shitty en suite. The door closes behind her and the lock clicks into place.

My back presses against the bathroom door and I squeeze my eyes shut. This is too hard; being around him is too hard. I thought I could make it back to New York and then figure out a plan, but who am I kidding? There is no plan for this because this is the only eventuality I couldn't possibly have predicted. I stare down at my flat stomach both horrified and mesmerized by the prospect. My head is telling me there is only one option here, that I need to go to a clinic and take care of it. But the heart I never had until a few weeks ago is hesitating, which is ridiculous. It's funny that when something is never even a possibility, you never think about it. And then when it's suddenly thrust in front of you, the reaction you might imagine yourself having never comes. I'm not so stupid as to think that I can have a baby. It's ridiculous. But, I've never done anything good in my life and probably never will. I bring death and destruction wherever I go. I can't stomach the thought of bringing death to something so innocent, something that defies all odds, and it makes me a hypocrite of the worst kind.

A plan starts to form in my mind and it's not ideal, but it's the best I have right now.

"Una," Nero calls from the other side of the door.

"Yeah?"

"I'm going to grab some food."

"Okay."

Now, it needs to be now. Once I'm in New York it will be harder, Nero will be around and if he's not then his men will be. As soon as I hear the motel room door slam, I move. I only have a small bag with me, with just enough clothes for a few days, some cash, a couple of burner phones and one gun. It's enough. For now. I throw on clothes and grab my stuff quickly. My hand is on the door-knob when I stop. I can't just leave him like this. I can't explain to him all the reasons why, but I can give him something.

I take a scrap of paper, letterhead with the motel's cheap looking logo. I hover with the pen over the paper for several moments. How do I say goodbye in a scribbled note? Nothing has changed and yet, everything has. He came for me, put his neck on the line, again, and now I'm leaving without so much as a word. Maybe I should just give him the truth. But then this is Nero. He's not the guy that has babies; he's the guy that puts a gun to their heads when their parents won't do what he wants. He doesn't need to know this.

Nero.

I can't stay with you. I know you would stand by me and fight the world if I asked you to, but this is my war and you shouldn't be a casualty of it. Take your power, live your life. Please keep Anna safe. I'll be back. I just have some things to take care of. Wait for me. Queen always protects king.

Una.

He'll believe that, and he'll let me run. I can't pretend

this isn't happening, and I can't just hope that Nero could deal with it. We aren't those people with the white picket fence and the normal lives. We're killers, depraved and motivated by the kinds of things that keep most people up at night. Everything is going to shit all at once. Time and space are what I need to figure it out without burdening him. This is on me, and it's best that way. When you rely on other people it only weakens you, and I can't afford weakness now.

Dropping the note on the bed, I hoist the duffel bag over my shoulder, leaving that run-down motel room without a backwards glance. As soon as I'm on the main road, I stick my thumb out, and it doesn't take long before a guy in a pickup truck pulls over.

"Where ya goin', sweetheart?" he says, tipping his cowboy hat back.

"The airport, please."

I'm now officially on the run. Let the chase begin.

To be continued in KISS ME. Available HERE.

OTHER BOOKS BY LP LOVELL

Sign up to my newsletter and stay up to date with new releases:

Join the Mailing List

Dark Mafia Series:

Kiss of Death series

Collateral Series

Touch of Death Series

Wrong Series

Bad Series

Standalones

Super Dark and Fucked Up:

Absolution

The Pope

The Game

Gritty High School Romance:

No Prince

No Good

Taboo Erotic Romance:

Dirty Boss

Website: www.lplovell.co.uk

Facebook: https://www.facebook.com/lplovellauthor

Instagram: @lp_lovell

TikTok: @authorlplovell

Goodreads: https://www.goodreads.com/author/show/
7850247.LP_Lovell

Amazon: https://www.amazon.com/LP-
Lovell/e/B00NDZ61PM

Made in the USA
Monee, IL
15 December 2022

21592834R10127